D0942579

SPECIAL MESSAGE TO READERS

This book is published under the auspices of

THE ULVERSCROFT FOUNDATION

(registered charity No. 264873 UK)

Established in 1972 to provide funds for research, diagnosis and treatment of eye diseases.

Examples of contributions made are: —

A Children's Assessment Unit at Moorfield's Hospital, London.

•

Twin operating theatres at the Western Ophthalmic Hospital, London.

•

A Chair of Ophthalmology at the Royal Australian College of Ophthalmologists.

•

The Ulverscroft Children's Eye Unit at the Great Ormond Street Hospital For Sick Children, London.

You can help further the work of the Foundation by making a donation or leaving a legacy. Every contribution, no matter how small, is received with gratitude. Please write for details to:

THE ULVERSCROFT FOUNDATION,
The Green, Bradgate Road, Anstey,
Leicester LE7 7FU, England.
Telephone: (0116) 236 4325

In Australia write to:

THE ULVERSCROFT FOUNDATION,
c/o The Royal Australian and New Zealand
College of Ophthalmologists,
94-98 Chalmers Street, Surry Hills,
N.S.W. 2010, Australia

WILDE COUNTRY

When Logan found he'd outlived his welcome in Mexico, he rode back north of the Rio, to reconcile himself with his father. But his father had died and there was no welcome from big brother Tate, whose alliance with a crooked attorney threatened to destroy the rest of the family. So, if Logan was to survive, and his kid sister and brother were to get what was due to them, he had to oil his guns — and use them!

Books by Tyler Hatch in the Linford Western Library:

A LAND TO DIE FOR
BUCKSKIN GIRL
LONG SHOT
DEATHWATCH TRAIL
VIGILANTE MARSHAL
FIVE GRAVES WEST
BIG BAD RIVER
CHEYENNE GALLOWS
DEAD WHERE YOU STAND!
DURANGO GUNHAWK
KNIFE EDGE

TYLER HATCH

WILDE COUNTRY

Complete and Unabridged

LINFORD
Leicester

First published in Great Britain in 2007 by
Robert Hale Limited
London

First Linford Edition
published 2009
by arrangement with
Robert Hale Limited
London

British Library CIP Data

Hatch, Tyler
Wilde country.—Large print ed.—
Linford western library
1. Western stories
2. Large type books
I. Title
823.9′14 [F]

ISBN 978–1–84782–585–8

Published by
F. A. Thorpe (Publishing)
Anstey, Leicestershire

Set by Words & Graphics Ltd.
Anstey, Leicestershire
Printed and bound in Great Britain by
T. J. International Ltd., Padstow, Cornwall

This book is printed on acid-free paper

1

Homeward Bound

Logan aimed to cross the river south of Del Rio but he had a hunch they were still on his trail.

There would be three — no, wait. Only two, because he was pretty sure his last shot had hit the fat one somewhere in his gross body; his size made him an easy target. That left Lewis and the Mexican — the one they called 'Razor', not because he favoured such a thing as a weapon but because his name was Arrezo; either way, he was a cold-blooded killer to be reckoned with.

Lewis was no slouch, either, and they still believed he had the sack of pesos and reales so there was no question that they would follow until they caught up.

Might as well get it over with — there

was some strange urge driving him back across the Rio and he wanted no more delays.

So he veered from the rocky country to arid land where it would be harder to hide his tracks. Neither Lewis nor Razor would be fooled if he left a plain trail. He would have to make it look like a botched attempt to cover his tracks.

It was easy enough to fake and once he was sure there was enough sign for them to figure he was making for the range of low hills lying north-west, he rode there at a fast clip. The distance was far enough for his smoke gelding, too; they had come a lot of miles since sundown two days ago after the shoot-out at Bella Mondo.

Logan glanced at the sky, squinting. The glare had been rasping his eyes since morning and he moistened the end of his neckerchief from his almost empty canteen, gently bathed away the grit and soothed the redness. It made some difference, enough for him to sight the hot Winchester well.

He hoped.

If he didn't stay on top of these two he was as good as dead. But even though he was expecting it, they still fooled him.

He had mortally wounded the fat one, all right, but they had brought him with them, roped him upright in the saddle with the aid of a sotol stick up his jacket at the back, and sent him into the ambush area, yelling and shouting behind as if all three were coming.

Weary, his eyes watering again and blurring his target, Logan spun around, saw the horse and rider and opened up. Three fast shots before he saw the dust spurting from the fat man's jacket and the arms flopping loosely. A fourth to put down the horse, lever clashing, waiting for Lewis or Razor to appear. One of them fired from behind a boulder down there and the lead whispered past his face. At the same time someone above and behind him shot him in the back.

It was a ricochet but cut across

beneath his shoulders like a searing branding-iron. Logan spun on to his back, rifle coming up and around. He saw the silhouette of the man above, thought it was Razor, but identity didn't matter. He put two shots into him, dust puffing from the dusty shirt. The Mexican lifted to his toes, took a wild, meaningless step forward and crashed down to land a few feet away.

Ignoring the pain across his back, Logan whirled, caught Lewis halfway up the slope, running well with his long legs, a sixgun in each hand. He saw Logan had spotted him and began firing, both guns spitting flame and smoke. Logan was concentrating so hard he didn't know — or care — where Lewis's lead went. As long as it didn't find him.

He planted his last three bullets into the middle of Lewis's chest and watched the man hurled back down the slope to sprawl unmoving at the bottom.

In celebration, he drank the last of

his water, mounted and rode for the distant Rio at a fast clip.

* * *

The escarpment stretched in a serrated arc all the way from Del Rio to Austin. Separating the hill country from the coastal plains, it ran in the general direction of the trail taken by the original settlers. Many — very many — once seeing the sweetwater springs and roaring streams, with the lush vegetation surrounding, cut their journey west and settled. There were plenty of fine sites for towns.

The one Logan was making for was called Cedar Butte.

It was a prosperous-looking town, a mix of clapboard and adobe buildings, with a couple of redbrick structures thrown in. The streets were wide, smoothed every second week by a heavy log road-roller and scraper, drawn by a specially imported team of four giant Clydesdales. There was a kind of plaza which many of the buildings faced; it had an ornate stone horse trough in the centre, shady trees planted around the edges of the roughly shaped square.

The town had advanced considerably since Logan was last here.

He recognized some of the business names painted on false-fronts and windows: Jarrold's General Store; McGee's Tonsorial Parlour, with, he reckoned, the same old striped red-and-white poles either side of the doorway; two saloons almost opposite each other, facing across the square: Mother Lode was still the same with fancy giltwork surrounding the name on a large streetfront window, but what used to be Ellison's was now called the Aces High — which sounded like they had finally legalized gambling in the town. And not before time.

He felt no great pleasure in returning, and yet there was something that seemed to make him relax — a bit, at any rate. Ah! New lawman — Sheriff Daniel F. Dalton, so the sign said in fancy script. The livery had extended.

He was tempted to turn in and stay overnight so the smoke could rest up, but his destination was only a few more miles.

So he let the animal drink at the ornate trough and then crossed the arched, stone-and-timber bridge over the river and headed past lines of houses and cabins that dwindled away into a few scattered shacks, well past the main town centre. He smiled thinly: looked as if the snooty folk who ran things hadn't changed any.

It was late afternoon before he topped the familiar rise which, long ago, he used to keep between him and the old ranch house before cutting away from the school track, making for where he had hidden his fishing pole near the creek . . .

The Block W wasn't the same ranch that he recalled.

At first he thought it was, but it was only the front of the old house; this had been extended, both sides and backwards. There was a tiled *galleria* running along the front and down two sides that he could see. More windows, too, with real glass in the frames flashing in afternoon light.

His gaze moved away from the huge house to the outbuildings. Two barns now, one as large as the original dwelling; looked like separate stables now, too. Four corrals, a good, solid smithy and forge instead of the old sheet-iron-and-bark affair, the humped earth of the root cellar now covered in flowers — planted, he figured, rather than wild. A couple of privies and a bunkhouse twice as large as he remembered.

There were men working around the yard and, way beyond, he saw riders and grazing herds of cattle on the Irish green slopes. He thumbed back his hat, revealing a thick thatch of sweat-matted brown hair through which he scratched at his scalp. *A much bigger crew than when he left* . . .

'I guess it's called 'progress',' he said to the totally uninterested smoke: the mount showed more interest in the corrals where many horses milled and others grazed on a fence pasture.

He felt a strange tightness forming in his belly as he heeled the smoke forward, towards the big gate with a swinging sign above on creaky chains: BLOCK W: VISITORS BY APPOINTMENT ONLY.

It had his elder brother's touch, that *By Appointment only*.

He wondered how hard Tate had had to work to talk the Old Man into such a sign.

Not that Marshall Wilde encouraged visitors, but he would never have been arrogant — or snobbish — enough to allow a sign like that without a fight.

Setting his hat square again, and wincing as the skin stretched on his back where the bullet wound had not yet healed completely, Logan Wilde rode towards the house where he had been born thirty years ago — and which he hadn't seen for seven of those years.

He couldn't help but wonder what kind of a welcome he was going to get.

In a matter of seconds he found out.

A man with a rifle stepped out from behind the old gnarled oak that had been there, just in from the gate, for as long as he could remember.

'You got your paper?' the man said, a big, beefy fellow about forty, craggy and looking like a fight would be as good as a bonus to him.

'Paper?'

'Your appointment . . . ' The cold, impatient emphasis suddenly stopped as the rifleman squinted. 'By the livin' saints! The Prodigal Son!'

'Thought it was you, Rio. You look just as mean as I recall — meaner if possible.'

'You ain't the fresh kid as rode outta here, bareback you was in so much of a hurry to leave, neither! How'd you find out?'

'Find out what?'

Rio frowned, then shook his head, thick lips twisting a little. 'Nah, nah.

Don't try that smart-mouth stuff with me, feller! You got away with a lot of it before but the Old Man ain't gonna protect you now!'

Logan felt his heart accelerate a little, sensing what was coming. 'Why's that?'

Rio studied him closely, then muttered something and said, 'You sayin' you don't know?'

'How about *you* quit the smart talk and tell me what the hell you're talking about?'

'Ah! Gotten kinda tough, eh? Well, I guess we all heard about that — some, leastways.' Face hard as an anvil, Rio said flatly: 'Old Marsh is dead; we buried him but a few weeks back.'

Logan tried to keep his face blank, but he was full of sudden, clawing tension; until Rio had hinted as much he hadn't given a thought to the Old Man's not still running Block W . . . Just didn't seem possible. 'Tate the new owner?' His voice was thick but he was damned if he was going to clear his throat right now.

'Uh-huh.' Rio made the sound very softly, the rifle still holding steady, mean eyes pinched down. 'I don't think he's gonna do cartwheels when he sees you.'

Logan shrugged; he and Tate had never gotten along, but then, there were few people Tate did get along with.

'How did the Old Man die?'

'In bed. You believe that? Man like him, active and raisin' hell all his life and he dies of blood poisonin'. Just drove a rusty nail into his hand. Coupla days later his hand was big as a steer's hind leg. Then he got a kind a lockjaw an' . . . Well, that's about enough, I reckon.' The rifle barrel jerked slightly. 'So how about you gimme down your guns and wait here while I go see if Tate wants to see you.'

'How about you just get outta my way?'

Rio grinned and Logan knew it was the kind of answer the man wanted. 'Yeah, seems like some of the things I heard about you just might be gospel.

But it don't change what I said. My orders are to stop anyone who don't have a written appointment.'

'You gonna stop me, Rio?'

'Already have.'

'Just temporarily.'

Logan jammed the spurs into the weary smoke's flanks and the horse, dozing during the talk, suddenly came to life and leapt forward instinctively. He wasn't close enough to ram into Rio but it startled the big man and he stepped hurriedly aside, stumbling. The horse crowded him then and when he staggered upright he was looking into the muzzle of Logan's Colt.

And the hammer spur was back under his thumb.

'Lose it, Rio. *Now!*'

Rio hesitated, eyes burning with hostility, and then he opened his hand and stepped away from the rifle as it clattered to the ground. Logan's gun barrel gestured for Rio to move further away. The smoke followed at Logan's command.

'Keep that crowbait away from me!'

Rio was back against the thick, gnarled bark of the tree trunk now. Logan deliberately turned the smoke side on and walked it into the big man, crushing him against the oak. Rio cussed and punched and Logan leaned forward and gunwhipped him across the head: his hat fell and was crushed under the stomping hoofs.

He moved the horse back and Rio collapsed, unconscious, a little blood running down from under the dark hair.

Logan holstered his sixgun, dismounted and picked up Rio's rifle. He mounted again and started for the house, working the lever of the rifle over and over again until the magazine was empty, the ejected shells glittering as they arced and fell randomly.

He tossed the Winchester into a bush and rode slowly on towards the big house, where he could see someone moving about on the *galleria*.

2

Nothing For You

'Don't bother stepping down, Logan. There's nothing for you here.'

The big man standing at the edge of the tiled gallery with a glass of some short, dark drink in one hand, stared coldly up at Logan still in the saddle of the smoke, one boot free of the stirrup as he prepared to dismount.

Logan swung the leg over the horse's back and stood beside the animal, holding the reins in his left hand. 'Nice that you still recognize me, Tate.'

Tate Wilde was flushed with anger. A couple of people behind him, in deep shadow, had stopped what they were doing to stare now. There was at least one woman there but Logan's eyes were still suffering from the glare and he couldn't make them out clearly in the deep shadows.

'I told you not to get off that horse.'

'I heard.'

Tate stepped out into the sunlight. Not eagerly.

Logan noticed the quality of the cream shirt and the striped trousers, the Mexican leather boots. Tate, knuckles white where they held the thick, patterned glass, took a sip of his drink, his grey eyes smouldering.

'We heard you were in Mexico. Selling your gun for *pesos*.'

'Seemed to be the only talent I had that could make me a living.'

'Then it's true! Well, thank God old Marsh never lived long enough to know that!' He took another sip, a bigger one this time, his gaze speculative now. 'You heard about the funeral, huh? Well, you arrived too damn late! And if you think there's a share of Block W waiting for you, mister, you are mighty mistaken!'

'Where'd they bury Pa?'

Tate Wilde frowned. He gestured vaguely with the now empty glass. 'Next to Ma, of course. Did you hear what I said about there being no share for you?'

'That's not why I came back. I never knew Pa was dead until Rio told me. Blood poisoning, he said.'

'Yeah! How'd you get by him?'

Logan shrugged just as there was a kind of wild whoop and the clatter of a racing horse. Rio came streaking into the yard on board his dun, yanked savagely on the reins, the horse's forelegs propping, hoofs skidding. He was out of the saddle before the animal had stopped, ducked behind it and ran at Logan, fists ready, streaks of sticky blood on his rage-contorted face.

'No son of a bitch gunwhips me and gets away with it!' Rio gritted as he swung his first blow.

'Tate! Stop them!'

It was a woman's voice from the shadowed gallery and Logan glanced there instinctively and next moment was sprawled on the ground, his jaw feeling as though it was around under his left ear, his head ringing. Rio bared his teeth as he stood over the downed man, fists knotted and cocked.

Logan rolled away from the boot that came towards him, twisted violently, wrenching open the bullet gouge across his back. But he didn't feel the skin splitting or the warm blood flowing. He bounced up into a crouch and Rio tried to lift a knee into his face. Logan Wilde stepped to one side, swung his right foot into Rio's thigh. Off balance, Rio tottered, staggered and despite a mighty effort to stay upright, went down to one knee.

Logan stepped in and slammed his right fist into the side of the man's head. His left was waiting, and as the blood-streaked face turned, Logan's knuckles crunched against the blubbery nose. Rio howled and went down, hands clawing at his face. Sobbing curses, he rolled instinctively away from Logan's advance, managed to stagger halfway upright, the tips of his fingers on his right hand against the ground. Then he charged forward from that position, roaring, arms spread wide like pincers, which he closed about Logan's body just above belt level.

Wilde felt the big hands lock behind his back and then he was eye-to-eye with Rio, the man's sour breath panting into his face as muscles strained and tried to to crush his ribs. Logan writhed, felt his breath going. Rio, sensing victory, leaned backwards with his effort, lifting Logan's feet clear of the ground for better purchase.

Mistake. Now Logan was free to swing his boots and he did so — one after the other, into Rio's unprotected shins, one kick high enough to crack on the guard's kneecap.

Rio stumbled as his leg started to fold up. His grip loosened and in a flash Logan's arms were free and he hammered another blow on to Rio's battered nose. The man lurched back, instinctively covering his face with both hands now, his eyes crossed.

Logan spread his boots, steadied, and hammered a volley of savage blows into the man's midriff. Rio gulped and retched, staggering backwards, arms flinging wide in his effort to retain balance.

Logan didn't give him a chance. He lunged after the man, swinging blow after blow into that thick body, jarring the guard from scalp to toenails. Rio started to lift a hand, maybe to signal he had had enough. Instead, Logan ducked under it swiftly. An uppercut that whistled chipped Rio's teeth as they clacked together violently. His legs buckled and Logan took a long step forward, right arm cocked back over his shoulder — but he stopped, didn't deliver the final blow.

Instead he placed a spread hand against the semi-conscious Rio's chest and pushed lightly. It was all that was needed. The gate guard fell loosely to the dust and lay there, bloody, snorting as he fought for breath before he slumped into unconsciousness.

Logan had to move his feet to retain his own balance, then he tore off his neckerchief and dabbed at the blood on his face. Without looking at Tate or those who had gathered on the gallery to watch the fight, he weaved his way to the horse trough, dipped his head in, then the neckerchief and mopped the cooling water over his face.

'Well, you were always a bit of a hellion, but I never thought I'd ever see you — or anyone else — take Rio.'

Vision blurred, one eye swelling rapidly, Logan squinted at Tate. He said nothing, went on mopping at his face which was red and lumpy where it wasn't smeared with blood. The back of his shirt was torn and also bloody.

'Seems you're a lot tougher since I last saw you.'

Still Logan didn't speak. He started to, but then he saw the woman he had glimpsed in the gallery's shadows moving up behind his elder brother. She likely would reach to his shoulder if she stood ramrod straight, had hair the colour of flax, caught up with some kind of Indian comb, showing her small pink ears and smooth neck. Her eyes were hazel and her face oval — and she was smiling. She ran past Tate and threw her arms about Logan.

'Oh, Logan! It's so good to see you! I wanted to run to you when we saw you riding in, but Tate wouldn't allow it, ordered me to stay back until he said different.'

She was looking defiantly at Tate and Logan frowned.

'Wouldn't *let* you?' He flicked his gaze from the girl to Tate. 'You're walking in Pa's footsteps, seems like, big brother: 'I speak, you obey!''

Tate lifted a hand, index finger straight and stiff as he poked it once in Logan's direction. 'Just remember that, *young* brother! I run the Block W now. I'm head of the Wilde family, not Pa — and what I say goes.'

Logan held his gaze on his brother and Tate's jaw sagged a little. Those eyes! It was as if Logan was sighting down the barrel of a gun pointed right at Tate.

'Pa left the ranch to you?'

'He did. Oh, Annie and Luke will get shares when they reach their majority, which is kind of a long wait for them, Luke being just sixteen and Annie not yet nineteen. But those are the terms of Pa's will and he named the executor as Ash McGowan — his family have been the Wilde's lawyers for a long time, as you'd likely recall.'

'I thought Pa fired him. McGowan tried to beat him out of that bottom land over by the Barton place.'

Tate made a sweeping gesture with one hand. 'Ah, Pa got it wrong. Barton's gone, anyway. His section is part of Block W now.' Recovering a little from his fright at seeing those killer eyes of Logan's, Tate said smugly, 'Afraid he never even mentioned you in his will, Logan.'

'Wouldn't expect him to.'

He looked down as he felt Annie's fingers squeeze his arm. She looked up into his battered face. 'He didn't hate you, Logan, but you . . . disappointed him, leaving like you did.'

Logan gave a small nod; he already knew that.

'Thought you'd be an old married woman by now, Annie. Nineteen! Why, you'll soon be doing needlework and making your own dresses, cooking up jams and cookies to fill in your time, generally acting like a true old maid if you don't hurry and find yourself a man.'

He spoke lightly but his words trailed off as her face crumbled, and the tears welled up in her eyes, her teeth tugging at her lower lip, before she whirled with a small sobbing sound and ran back under the gallery. Moments later he heard a door slam. He frowned as he looked at Tate.

'What did I say?'

'Oh, just stirred a little problem between Annie and me. You don't have to concern yourself with it.'

'She's my kid sister. What makes her unhappy is my concern.'

'Not when you quit the family the

way you did. Told you: I'm the big *jefe* here now. I make the decisions for the whole family.'

'Not for me, you don't.'

Tate's face straightened. 'You no longer count, Logan,' he said coldly. 'Can't you get that through your head? *We don't want you here!* Now you can tend to your horse and wash up properly behind the northern bunk-house, then be on your way. It'll be best for everyone if you don't come here again.'

Logan studied the man and then snorted gently. 'You won't let Annie have the man she wants, is that it?'

Tate flushed. 'I told you, it's no business of yours! Now, are you going? Or do I have to call some of the men to see you off Block W?'

He jumped back as Logan's sixgun suddenly appeared in his younger brother's hand. Tate's eyes widened, then Logan smiled thinly, held the hammer spur under his thumb while he inspected the cylinder, turning it to check the loads. Still smiling crookedly, he holstered the gun and heard Tate's held breath whistle through his teeth. He looked mighty pale.

'Relax, Tate. Just checking my gun in case I need it — along the trail, I mean.'

Tate swallowed. 'You — you've sure changed!'

'You haven't — which is too bad.' Logan led his horse to the trough and set about washing trail dust and dried foam from the smoke.

He was aware of eyes watching him as he took the horse into the stables he had never seen before. They were large and there was some mighty fine — and expensive — horseflesh in the stalls. One of the men working there — he didn't know any of them — started to come towards him, then changed his mind and went on with his chores as Logan curry-combed his mount and gave it a nosebag of oats.

By the time he was ready to wash-up himself Rio had gone, and some of the cowhands were arriving back for supper. He was sluicing water over his face when he heard a step behind him, whirled, Colt sweeping up.

'Whooo-eeeee!' exclaimed the youth standing there, a tentative smile on his face. 'I never seen anyone draw that fast before, Logan!'

Logan frowned, holstering the gun. 'Luke? Judas, boy, you've growed! You were still in knee-pants when I left!'

'I — I'm sixteen now.' Luke hesitated, then stepped forward, holding out his right hand.

Logan smiled and clasped. Luke said 'Ouch!' rubbed his hand after he broke the grip. Logan tousled the tow-head roughly but fondly, felt the boy's upper arm through the shirt. 'Good to see you, Luke. Got some muscles working-up there.'

Luke nodded, his smile fading. 'Tate sees I get plenty of what he calls . . . exercise.'

'Got you working the spread?'

The boy nodded. 'Tate says I gotta know how from the bottom up. I've had my fill of cleaning out the barns and stables and corrals. Broke an arm first time I tried breaking-in a mustang . . .'

Logan swore softly. 'He put you on a raw mustang? A lightweight like you!'

Luke shrugged, looking a little apprehensive now at Logan's disapproving tone. 'Well, even before Pa died, Tate was running things. Pa was just too old, I guess. We have to do what Tate says. I know I have to learn everything. Part of the ranch'll be mine some day.'

Logan didn't say anything for a short time, then nodded jerkily. 'Well, Tate's the eldest and Pa left the spread to him. I guess you gotta obey him for a few years yet. But mebbe he needs to go about things differently.'

Luke snorted. 'I wouldn't try to tell him that! Tate's more stubborn than Pa ever was. When he makes up his mind — '

'I stick to it!' snapped Tate Wilde, coming ground the corner of the bunkhouse. He glared at Luke. 'I told you to stay in your room until Logan had left.'

'I — I just wanted to say howdy, Tate! It's been years since we seen him . . . '

Tate cuffed him lightly. 'Go in and get your supper.' He looked challengingly at Logan. He was carrying one of his cream shirts and tossed it at Logan who instinctively caught it. 'Yours is a mess. Put it on and you'll be ready to go.'

'I was. But now I dunno.' Logan shrugged into the comfortable shirt. It fit him pretty well. 'Thanks for the shirt.'

Tate ignored the remark. 'You're going! Told you, there's nothing for you here.'

'I'm not so sure. Annie — Luke — you're bullying the hell outta them.'

Tate stepped back, looked around the corner and nodded. Three men appeared: two Logan knew from before; Birch and Hollis, tough cowhands. The third was a slat of a man with a narrow, mean face. He was the one with the shotgun. The other two had rifles. Tate smiled crookedly.

'Time for you to go, Logan. The boys'll see you off Block W land. Just in case you've forgotten the trail out after all this time . . . If we never meet again, it'll be too soon.'

'It'll be more than that.'

Tate's face straightened and he looked uncertain, then hardened his jaw, just like old Marsh Wilde used to.

'Get him out of here! Make sure he doesn't come back!'

He swung away and strode across towards the main house.

As the armed trio escorted him away from Block W, Logan looked back when they reached the rise and thought he saw a pale face at an upstairs window. The curtains dropped back before he could identify it.

But he was pretty sure it was Annie.

3

Neighbour

The slat-like man was called Splinter. He was a sour type, had watery eyes, half-hooded by droopy lids. Logan figured he must be seeing just half of the world, but maybe that was enough for Splinter. He rode a little aside from Birch and Hollis, dropped back after a few miles as the sun began to slide behind the hills.

Birch moved up on Logan's right, Hollis on his left.

'What happened to your back?' Birch asked. Birch was a hard-muscled veteran cowhand he remembered as being something of a Saturday-night troublemaker. Sheriff Keene had usually tossed him in the cells to sleep off the drink.

'Cut myself shaving.'

Hollis, a little older than Birch, guffawed, bared his gums in a smile; he only put his set of dentures in at meal times. He slapped a thigh. 'By jingo, Logan, you ain't changed much! Just as sassy as when you was a kid.'

Birch scowled. 'Man asks a civil question, gets a mouthful of smart! No call for that.'

'Don't whine, Birch. I know damn well what Tate told you to do.'

'That so? Never knew there was any gypsy in the Wilde blood that'd let you read minds!'

'You just never know with us Wildes, Birch. Ain't you learned that in all the years you've worked for Block W?'

'Listen, you had the Old Man to protect you before when you raised hell but he's gone now. Tate don't want you around. And damned if we do, neither!'

'You speak for all the hands?'

Birch grinned and waved a hand. 'Us three're all that matters right now, far as you're concerned, Logan.'

'How much further?' called Splinter

from behind, still carrying the shotgun across his thighs. He sounded impatient.

Logan hipped in the saddle, slowing the smoke, but Birch slapped its rump with his hat and growled at him to keep going at a faster pace. Logan looked into Splinter's axe-blade face, saw the meanness there, the way the man's hand steadying the shotgun opened and closed around the shiny blue steel barrels.

Surely Tate hadn't ordered him killed! He expected them to try a beating, but murder? No! Tate wasn't like that. But it had been seven years since he'd last seen him.

Logan had learned long ago it was better to take steps to prevent something that might happen, than let it happen and then find out it was too late to stop it.

Splinter didn't like the bleak look on Logan's face. An edgy man, sensitive about his gauntness, with little conscience, he saw Logan's look as a challenge.

With a twist of his thin lips, he suddenly raised the shotgun in a blur. Birch yelled, 'Christ, don't!' and wrenched his mount roughly aside. Hollis was already spurring away, leaving Logan exposed and alone.

Splinter didn't hear or see any of it; he was concentrating on Logan Wilde. As the hammer cocked under his thumb he felt the familiar old surge of excitement and pleasure that came when he was about to kill.

The smoke reacted to the touch of Logan's spurs with a leap to the side and upslope. Logan slid partway out of the saddle, left hand clinging to the horn, reins trailing free. His Colt came up in his right hand and blazed across the moving horse.

Splinter jerked, lifted up out of the saddle as the shotgun exploded and killed the horse under him, the buckshot taking it in the back of the head. There was a welter of animal and human limbs thrashing. Splinter skidded down the slope, hit, without the shotgun now, but dragging his sixgun free. Logan's Colt barked again and Splinter's thin body spun across the slope, sliding more slowly now, the gun falling from nerveless fingers.

Still riding upslope, clinging to one side of the saddle, Logan fired at Birch and Hollis. Both men had guns in their hands, ducked instinctively.

'Hold it! *Hold it*!' yelled Birch. 'Judas priest, Logan, we ain't gonna kill you!'

'I can guarantee that.' Logan heaved up into the saddle and reined down, turning the smoke to face the cowhands. The horse was breathing hard, was feeling the effects of the long arduous ride since crossing the Rio. Logan patted its head and held the Colt on the two cowboys.

Birch glanced at Hollis and nodded. They holstered their guns and lifted their empty hands out in front of them.

'Tate just wanted you . . . beat up a little. Makin' sure you savvied he meant it when he said he din' want you back on Block W.'

'So he chose you two and that walking cadaver.'

'He ain't walkin' now,' Hollis said, showing his gums again. 'An' never will. You got yourself some trouble, boy. Sheriff Dalton don't like dead men with bullets in 'em in his county.'

'You two saw it was self-defence.'

The Block W hands glanced at each other. Birch licked his lips. 'Aw, we got nothin' agin you, Logan. You was a pain in the ass when you was younger, figured you were mighty important because your old man owned the ranch and that you could get away with just about anythin'.'

'Damn well did, too!'

Logan gave a faint smile. 'Guess I was trying to impress Pa. Knew it was a losing battle. He seemed to favour Tate every time I got into a scrape. Still, most times he did help.'

'That true about you bein' a gunfighter across the Rio?'

'I was a lot of things across the Rio. I had a few gunfights.'

'I b'lieve it!' Hollis said. 'The way you shot old Splinter outta the saddle!'

Logan gestured with his gun. 'Better drape him over one of your mounts. Damn fool killed his own . . . No, wait.' He swung down out of the saddle. 'Old Smoke's not doing too well, but I like that sorrel of yours. We'll swap. Put my saddle on your mount and you take the smoke.'

'Hell! Tate'll have my neck, swapping the sorrel for that crowbait!'

'That 'crowbait' has carried me hundreds of miles. He's earned a rest.' Logan's voice hardened as Birch took the saddle off the smoke. 'Could be I'll be back sometime, Birch. And that horse better have been treated right.'

Birch swallowed and heaved his own saddle on to the weary smoke. 'You're a damn fool if you come back, Logan.'

'Mebbe. But you just remember it's a possibility and take damn good care of the smoke.'

Birch swallowed and nodded jerkily; he didn't aim to cross the Logan Wilde who had returned to Wilde Country.

Then he and Hollis began arguing about who would carry Spinter's corpse back to Block W headquarters.

Logan glanced at the sky, colour-painted now by the sinking sun. 'You do it, Hollis. Carrying Birch'll be enough for the smoke. Me, I aim to find a good camping-place before dark. So long.'

They watched him turn the big sorrel uphill and ride to the crest. He paused and looked back and Birch cupped one hand to his mouth and called,

'You better stay clear of Wilde country, Logan! Tate's got big plans — an' you ain't part of 'em.'

Logan turned and rode over the crest without a word or a gesture.

* * *

He found a good camping-place in a small gulch on the north slope. Grass, a trickle of a creek, overhanging trees for shelter. And down here, a small campfire would not be readily seen.

Logan was pretty sure he was now off Block W, but he knew that the ranch had expanded a lot since he had last seen it and figured there was a possibilty he might still be on Wilde land. So he took more precautions with his cooking fire, digging a hollow first and edging it with deadfall timber to shield the flames and any glow.

It was likely Tate would send someone to make sure he wasn't camping on Block W land.

But he spent a peaceful night and hurried to light his fire come morning, rubbing his hands together and spreading his palms to the growing flames. It was mighty chilly up here, a little mist lay in a hollow below him.

He was setting the battered coffee pot to heat over the flames at one side when suddenly it jerked and spun away wildly, spurting water and coffee grounds from the brand-new hole in the side.

About .44 calibre.

The rifle shot cracked and echoed

around the slope. He was belly-down behind a deadfall when a second shot sent pieces of bark above his shoulders hurtling violently into the air. The bullet hummed away in ricochet. Three more rapid shots sprayed him with more bark, making him keep his head down, swearing.

Then two more shots and, when he eased his head up he was startled to see that the sorrel's reins had been cut through. By a bullet? The horse reared back, whinnying. It would have run down the gulch, except for the hobbles he had put on last night to make sure it didn't wander back to the distant ranch. The next shot took his hat off. *That was too damn close!*

Three more deliberate shots tore up his bedroll, sent his grubsack spinning, and there was a ringing clunk as his canteen hurtled across the grass, blasted open by a bullet.

Logan grew more and more frustrated as he crouched behind his log, gun in hand. His hat was lying behind him on the ground, a bullet hole through the crown. The cream shirt was stained with grass juices and smears of dirt.

If he could just see the damn rifleman . . .

Then there was shadowy movement in the veil of mist as someone stepped into the clear, and he lifted his Colt, thumbing the hammer back.

But he held his fire.

The shooter was a young woman and she brought her smoking rifle up to her shoulder.

'I can shoot the eye out of a lizard at a hundred paces! It'll be easy to put a bullet into you — at any place I choose.'

Logan frowned, held up his gun hand, hammer lowered now. Slowly, warily, he stood up and holstered the Colt, then lifted his hands shoulder high. He was more curious than worried. 'I ain't gonna argue with you, ma'am.'

'Then you have better sense than I

gave you credit for. You must be new to Block W.'

'Don't work there, lady. I'm just passing through.'

'Well, that's as may be, but I've seen Tate Wilde wear shirts like that, and you're on my land. I'm within my rights to shoot trespassers. Walk on down here, holding your hands just where they are.'

The rifle barrel lifted just a fraction and he sighed, started down the slope, hands raised, turning sideways for better footing. She stopped him when he reached the end of the gulch, about five yards from her.

She was somewhere in her twenties, he estimated. A redhead with green eyes but no freckles showing, as he might have expected. Her skin looked smooth and tanned from outdoors. Her clothes told him she was a working landowner, anyway: worn riding-boots with tarnished spurs, stained denim trousers, a faded green shirt with the corner of the pocket sagging. Her hat showed signs of weathering, too, as did the gloves that covered her small hands — and now held the rifle she seemed mighty familiar with and at ease holding on him.

Suddenly her face changed; perhaps it was a little on the narrow side but with an attractive mouth and nose. The eyes narrowed, after first widening just a fraction. She licked at her lips.

'My God! You're one of them! Not just some drifter.'

'I've done a power of drifting, ma'am. What am I 'one of'?'

'The damn Wilde clan! You look like old Marsh with the wrinkles ironed out, and I can see a lot of Tate there, too.'

'I'm Logan Wilde.'

She nodded slowly. 'The wild Wilde! I've heard of you. Ran away years ago — some said to escape trouble.'

She waited but he didn't reply. The rifle didn't waver an inch.

'Ain't your arms getting tired?'

'Not so I'd notice. What're you doing here on my land?'

He lowered his arms slowly; she didn't protest, though she watched him mighty closely. 'When I was here before, this was all open range.'

'Yes. Your father apparently didn't want this area. When he decided he could use it after all, I'd already bought and proved-up, and had it in the land register. Not that that stopped him! He used a lawyer named McGowan to try and find a loophole that would force me to leave.'

'I guess it didn't work. But didn't he offer to buy you out? That's the way he'd do things.'

'He made a ridiculous offer, as you'd expect. Well, maybe *you* wouldn't but anyone living in this county wouldn't be surprised.'

Logan was silent for a few moments, his face unreadable. 'You know my name — what's yours?'

She hesitated, then answered, lowering the rifle at last but still holding it down in front where she could swing it in his direction in a split second.

'Valerie Guthrie. Owner of the V-Bar-G. *And* enemy of Block W — and anyone connected with it.'

Logan pursed his lips. 'Tate been giving you a hard time, I guess.'

'He's arrogant. Greedy. He already owns half the range. Why he wants my section I fail to understand.'

'You'd have to understand Tate.'

She looked at him curiously. 'Do I hear a touch of hostility there?'

He smiled. 'Just a touch. Tate doesn't want me at Block W. I was riding clear of the ranch when I camped here. There's a fence back there, hasn't been maintained too well. My horse was able to step over the wire without my having to dismount. Thought I'd crossed the line to open range.'

Val Guthrie studied him a little longer, hesitated, then lowered the rifle. He noticed she kept a finger on the trigger and thumb on the hammer spur.

'I don't know why I should believe you, but . . . No one would ever mistake you for anything but a Wilde, yet you seem . . . different.' Then she smiled suddenly. 'Ah! Wait! I think I see it now. You weren't given a share in old Marsh's will! And you resent it. Is that it?'

'I wasn't given a share, didn't expect one. No resentment. Fact, didn't even know Pa had died.'

Her green gaze looked him up and down. 'You don't look to me like a man who would leave just because his big brother told him to. Your reputation has preceded you.'

She jumped as he slapped a hand against the lower part of his holster, her rifle snapping up, but all he said was,

'You mean this? Likely exaggerated.'

Scepticism crossed her face. 'Are you trying to tell me you're not a gunfighter?'

'Not like Hickok or John Wesley Hardin, no. I've had several gunfights, but didn't go looking for them, except maybe twice.' He paused. 'Personal scores to settle.'

'There's a lot of gossip comes across

the Rio. Even if only half of what they say about you is true . . . '

If she expected an answer she didn't get one. For the first time, she looked uncertain and he said,

'You've wrecked my gear, even my canteen. Guess I'll have to make a detour to town for new stuff before I move on.'

'You still had no right to camp here!' No give or repentance there. The rifle moved towards the crest of the range. 'Ride that way and you'll cut the trail to town on the far side. I'll wait.'

He shook his head slowly, a faint smile on his lips.

When he had gathered what could be salvaged from his gear and had mounted he poked a finger through the bullet hole in his hat. 'Most comfortable hat I ever had.' He put it on, glaring. 'You'll likely hear another story about me pretty soon. Me and a feller called Splinter.'

Her shoulders stiffened a little. 'That — killer? What's happened to him?'

'Keep your ear to the ground,' he said and turned the sorrel up the slope.

She watched him go, rifle sagging now, a frown pulling her pale eyebrows closer together.

4

Man With a Star

Jarrold's General Store had everything he wanted, though it left his pockets almost empty.

'Don't suppose I could put it on Block W's account?'

Jarrold was a pleasant enough man, grey-haired — what there was of it — and ruddy-faced, with a waistline that kept him from getting too close to his counter and shelves. He smiled at Logan's query.

'If I was sure you were staying or working there . . . '

Logan nodded and paid for his parcels.

'I'm sorry. But — well, I'm sure Tate would fuss if I were to do as you suggest. Your brother is a powerful man, aligned as he is with Ash McGowan.'

Logan frowned, nodded. 'Thanks

anyway.' He picked up the parcels, four in all, unwrapped the canteen and slung it across his chest so he could better handle the other three. He turned to leave and stopped in his tracks.

A lean man just under six feet stood blocking his exit. Not that Logan took much notice of the man's size; his attention was caught by the brass star pinned to his shirt, vest open just enough to see it. 'I'm the sheriff.'

Logan arched his eyebrows; the man was younger than he had expected, thought him a deputy at first, but saw the word 'Sheriff' engraved on the star.

'Daniel F. Dalton,' Logan said and the man nodded soberly. 'I read the sign.'

He had a pleasant enough face, a little heavy around the jaw line and his nose had felt a fist or two in the past. There were a few scars above his eyebrows, too. Logan's gaze dropped a little: the lawman wore only one gun, very low, tied down with rawhide to his thigh. His hand brushed the butt as he stood there.

'You're Logan Wilde? Thought so. Like you to come along to my office.'

Logan tensed slightly. 'Now?'

'If it's convenient.'

Logan smiled thinly. 'And if it's not?'

Dalton shrugged. 'We'll go anyway.'

They left the store together, Dalton even taking one of Logan's parcels which he carried in his left hand.

There was a low fence of varnished wood with a swing-gate separating the desk and gun cabinets and other cupboards from the public part of the law office. Dalton motioned to a chair and went through the gate to sit behind his desk. 'You know why you're here.'

'I do?'

'Don't smart-talk me, Logan! I know you Wildes think you run this county, but one day it's going to sink in that I'm the law here and any respect I feel I'm due has been hardly earned. And I will have it or someone will wish they'd never been born.'

Logan studied the man. He was hostile, angry, but his face hadn't changed and he spoke evenly enough. It was his hands that gave him away; they gripped the edges of his desk so that the knuckles showed white. His breathing was audible, too, and one foot that Logan could see through the rails was gently tapping the floor.

'I'm a Wilde by birth, but I have nothing to do with Block W.'

'I imagine Tate would've seen to that!' Dalton's words were almost gritted now, his eyes narrowing. 'Yeah. I heard he wasn't pleased to see you. It didn't stop him reporting that you'd shot and killed one of his men. In fact, he seemed pleased to do it — upstanding citizen and so on.'

'Not in your opinion.'

Muscles showed along Dalton's jawline as his eyes bored into the man sitting across from him. His fingers tapped and then he sat back in his chair, holding the arms.

'Stay with this man Splinter you killed.'

Logan told him what had happened, adding, 'Tate didn't see fit to send in either Birch or Hollis?' The sheriff shook his head. 'Well, wouldn't really expect him to. But they were witnesses when Splinter tried to shoot me with a sawed-off shotgun. He was careless and killed his own horse with it. You ride out, you can see for yourself. If the coyotes have left enough.'

After a long minute, Dalton stood up. 'I saw Birch going into the saddler's earlier. He might still be there. But I want to get his story without you being there. Can I trust you to stay put until I get back?'

'I've got nowhere special to go.'

Dalton still hesitated, then apparently made up his mind, came through the gate and went to the street door. 'I shouldn't be long.'

'I'll be here.'

Dalton was back in fifteen minutes and came in with his right hand resting on the butt of his lowslung Colt. He didn't show surprise when he saw Logan lounging in his chair, smoking. But maybe there was a touch of relief,

Wilde thought. Maybe.

Sitting behind his desk again, Dalton said, 'Birch backs your story. It was self-defence. I'll check with Hollis later. You and Tate don't get along too well, I hear.'

'Seven years since I've seen him. He's had to work the spread all that time. To his way of thinking, I haven't earned a share.'

'And you think you have?'

Logan shook his head. 'Don't care. I came back to see the Old Man. Didn't know he was dead. Tate said I wasn't mentioned in the will and that didn't surprise me.'

'But he kicked you off just the same.' Sheriff Dalton tightened his lips and shook his head slowly. 'He's an arrogant son of a bitch.'

He looked slantwise at Logan: maybe he was testing him. Trying for some reaction.

'You won't get an argument from me about that.'

Dalton stared for a long time and

Logan was about to ask if he could go when the man said,

'I want to marry your sister.'

Logan blinked. The admission took him by surprise.

'So you're the one. I figured there was someone the way Annie acted. And that Tate had poked his nose in.'

Grim-faced, Dalton nodded. 'Nothing we can do. She's underage. He's legally head of the family. If he won't give his permission — '

'You know why?'

'I . . . No, I don't know why! I have a good steady job here. It's not a rip-roaring trail town and what troubles we do have are never too big for me to handle.'

'So far.'

'I'm not worried about that part.'

Logan liked the man's confidence. 'Maybe Tate's worried you might get killed and leave Annie a widow.'

Dalton frowned deeper. 'You taking sides with Tate?'

'Just wagging my jaws. I think Annie

should marry who she wants.' His grey eyes snapped and took on a bleak look momentarily. 'Provided he's a decent man and aims to treat her right.'

'By God, I do that! I'm building a small house out by the river. Just clapboard, but it'll be fine for Annie and me. We can extend when there's . . . children.' He flushed suddenly, dropped his gaze, fiddled with the edge of a pile of papers. 'I truly love her, Wilde.'

He saw Dalton was embarrassed and knew why: a tough lawman used to handling drunks and brawling cowboys, suddenly admitting to sentiment — and to a stranger at that.

'Then if Annie loves you back, I don't see the problem.'

Dalton's fist smashed down on to the desk. 'Problem? Are you crazy — or just dumb! I told you Tate won't give his approval and he has the legal right! *That*'s the problem.'

Logan stood and Dalton's gaze followed his movements warily. 'Yeah.

Tate's a problem to just about everyone. But you and Annie could always elope.'

The sheriff snorted. 'Think I haven't thought about that? Hell, like I said, I've a good job here but I'd throw it up in a minute if Annie would come away with me.'

'You've asked her?'

'Twice. She's scared white of Tate. Also — well, she says she's earned her share of Block W and it's her due. I'm not interested in that. I want to look after her myself, provide for her. I'm no rancher, but she won't budge. I think what she really wants is to get on the same footing as Tate, kind of square up to him, to have a say in things. Legally . . . Aw, I dunno. But she is scared to run.'

Logan picked up his parcels, looking thoughtful.

'I guess I'm free to go?'

Dalton smiled crookedly. 'I'm kinda glad Birch backed your story. I've heard about you and wasn't looking forward to having to throw you in jail.'

On impulse he thrust out his right hand and Logan juggled the parcels, gripped with him.

'You seem all right to me, Dalton.'

The sheriff seemed surprised. 'Well — thanks! What'll you do now?'

'Drift, I guess. Maybe look around the country, see how it's changed.'

Dalton was sober now, had an 'official' look. 'I'd stay away from Block W if I was you. I have enough trouble with Tate now.'

Logan smiled faintly and went out into the sunlight and noise of Main Street.

He tied his parcels on to the sorrel and was about to mount when a sign caught his eye across the street.

Ashley McGowan
Attorney-at-Law

Logan wrapped the reins about the hitch rail and walked across. There was a set of stairs at the side of the building with a smaller sign in the shape of an arrow, bearing McGowan's name again, pointing upwards.

He went in through the door at the top of the landing. There was a small reception area with a grey-haired matronly woman pecking laboriously at one of those typing machines he had heard about. Beyond was McGowan's office, marked PRIVATE.

Logan touched his hand to his hat-brim. '’Mornin’, Miss Harper. You're looking well.'

She adjusted her half-moon glasses and stared at him. Her mouth tightened a little but she replied levelly enough. 'Thank you, Mr Logan. I'm sorry I can't say the same for you. You look positively . . . ' she allowed herself a small smile, adding, 'wild. Altogether different from Mr Tate.'

'He's the rich one of the family.' He gestured towards the 'Private' door. 'Ash busy?'

'Mr McGowan is always busy,' she told him haughtily and he noticed the kind of hushed reverence when she mentioned McGowan's name: it had been part of local gossip seven years ago that she carried a torch for Ash McGowan, but he had never noticed or simply hadn't done anything about it. Logan had always felt a little sorry for her. 'We have three clerks in the back room and we could really do with one or two more. We are *very* busy, so Mr McGowan cannot be disturbed.'

Logan nodded, knowing he was going to get the run-around. So he stepped over the low rail and entered the area. Miss Harper leapt to her feet, outraged.

'Mister Logan! You may have been absent for some years but you ought to know better — '

'I do. But I'm in a hurry, Miss Harper.' He smiled thinly, placed a hand on the inner office door. 'I'll see McGowan doesn't blame you.'

'No, no! You mustn't. You can't just . . . '

But he was through and the door clicked closed behind him. Ash McGowan sat behind his desk, smoking a fragrant cigar, a prosperous-looking gent, with the cold eyes of a man who regards money as the most important thing in life. Steel-grey hair, mutton chops of a darker colour, a nourished face and body, immaculate in Eastern-bought clothes.

His eyes narrowed and his mouth sagged slightly before he snapped, 'What're you doing in here?'

'Come to see you, Ash.' Logan dropped into a padded leather visitor's chair and started a little when a man moved away from the window which was bright with sun glare. It was Rio, his face showing evidence of their last meeting.

'I'll throw him out, Ash.'

He started forward but McGowan held up a hand. 'Wait. He's here now.' He smiled coldly at Logan. 'I imagine it's something to do with the will, so I'll tell you right now, you do not get a mention, and certainly have no claim on a share of Block W.'

'So Tate told me — several times. That's OK. But I'd like to see a copy of the will Old Marsh left.'

McGowan was already shaking his head. 'Not possible. It can be of no possible interest to you.'

'You're wrong there. I'm mighty interested in it.'

'I am under no obligation to show it to you, Logan. You are not mentioned as a beneficiary or in any other way.'

Logan kept his face expressionless. He wasn't surprised Marshall Wilde hadn't left him a share, or anything else, but he felt certain sure the irascible old rancher would have had something final to say about the son who, in his eyes, deserted him and his obligations to the Wilde family. The Old Man had always had the last word and he would make sure his feelings about Logan were clearly known.

Logan flicked his eyes to Rio. 'What interest does he have in the will?'

McGowan's heavy eyebrows arched. 'Rio? None at all. He is here on other business, to do with Block W.' The lawyer smiled thinly. 'Another area where you lack interest.'

'Ash, I might not have any legal claim on Block W and that doesn't worry me. But I still have 'interest' in the ranch — and those who live there, particularly Annie and Luke. I intend to make sure they get their rightful share.'

McGowan sighed. 'It's spelt out quite plainly in the will. I am executor and will see that all legal requirements are met. So you can cease worrying about it, Logan, and I'd be pleased if you would leave. I have some important affairs to discuss with Rio.'

Logan flicked his eyes to the Block W ramrod. 'Well, I guess Rio always was a giant of intellect. Tate must trust the hell out of him to let him handle his business. And you.'

McGowan rose swiftly. 'Now that is *enough*! Rio, will you please see Logan off the premises?'

Logan shifted his gaze to the ramrod and was mildly surprised to see Rio holding his sixgun on him, smiling crookedly. 'Be a pleasure, Ash!'

Logan nodded to McGowan. 'I'll be seeing you, Ash.'

The lawyer frowned as he sat down and Rio marched Logan through the reception area. Miss Harper straightened in her chair, her worried face now showing surprise. Logan opened the door on to the landing and he caught the anticipation on the ramrod's face; his suspicions confirmed as Rio said,

'Watch them steps, they're mighty steep.'

Rio was already lifting the gun to club Logan, who stepped back the last few inches against the railing, slapped the descending gun aside, and kicked Rio's legs out from under him. The ramrod yelled, dropped his gun, snatched wildly at the rail but missed by a foot. He tumbled and crashed and bounced his way to the bottom where he lay stunned, bloody, clothes torn. Logan walked down slowly and stood over the dazed man.

'You're right, Rio. Those stairs are dangerous.'

5

Wilde Country

Tate Wilde looked across the bunk-house at his foreman as Rio sat on the edge of his bunk. His face was bruised and swollen. There was a plaster above one eye and along one side of his jaw. His left hand was bandaged and he moved with obvious pain, limping noticeably after returning from town.

Tate didn't show much sympathy. 'And has he gone? I mean really gone?'

'Hell, Tate, I dunno! Judas, man, he threw me down McGowan's stairs! I'm lucky I can still walk.'

'Reckon you are. You're not shaping up too good against my little brother, are you, Rio?'

'Little? The son of a bitch is strong as a grizzly an' fast as a rattler. I dunno what he's been doin' the last seven years, but he's no one to tangle with now!'

Tate lit a cheroot, tossed the slim packet to Rio and they both lit up. 'Logan was always one for details. Wanted to know how things worked and why. Used to drive the Old Man crazy with his questions sometimes. I didn't care — the more he riled Old Marsh the better for me.' His mouth hardened and his eyes took on a faraway look. 'The Old Man worked the tripe outta me, but favoured Logan, despite all his complaints. I could see it; knew he had Logan in mind to manage things, just use me for the sweat-and-muscle party. He got Logan outta quite a few scrapes, including that last one that was supposed to put an end to things.'

Rio smiled with his swollen mouth. 'Yeah, well we both know about that, don't we?'

Tate's eyes narrowed. 'We do, and long as both of us know, you have a job — and it's time you earned your money, Rio.'

‘Damn well thought I was! Look at me, for Chris’sake!’

‘I guess you — being the unforgiving soul you are — would be keen to square with Logan?’

Rio snorted and immediately winced.

‘We have to make sure he leaves this neck of the woods.’

‘Or stays here — permanent!’

Tate frowned, holding up a hand. ‘I don’t want it to go that far. Not yet, anyway. If Annie suspected anything — and she cares a helluva lot for Logan — she’d tell that damn sheriff she wants to marry! I know they meet somehow. I don’t want a goddamn lawman anywhere near this place, let alone as a member of the family.’

‘So that makes Logan lucky!’

‘For now. You won’t be much good doing your chores around the place for a few days. Take a break. Maybe go for a long ride through the ranges. Make sure there’re no strange riders hanging about. You know there’s been some rustling in the county.’

Rio digested this. 'S'pose I find a rider — but he's no stranger?'

'If he has no genuine business, see him on his way.'

'Might need a little help.'

'Pick a couple of men. Not Birch or Hollis. But you may run into them out on the range. I'm not happy that they backed up Logan's story of self-defence against Splinter.'

Rio smiled again. 'Sure. I savvy. Guess a little gentle exercise'll do me good. Stop my muscles stiffenin' up.'

Tate nodded and stood to leave. Rio cleared his throat. 'I gotta pay the sawbones for stitchin' the cut over my eye and along my jaw.'

Door halfway open, Tate looked steadily at Rio. 'All right. I'll take care of it. It's a reasonable expense, incurred while doing a chore for me. But I wouldn't want too many more.'

Rio merely nodded and Tate slammed the door after him.

The ramrod blew a long breath. It hurt his mouth but he didn't care. He would have to watch his step with Tate, not push him too far, too fast — but he figured he had a lot more coming to him than he was getting.

Aloud, he said to the empty bunkhouse, 'And I'll make damn sure I get every cent I'm due.'

* * *

The three riders on the rim watched Logan on the narrow trail far below in a canyon north-west of the ranch house.

They hadn't expected to find him so far out and had ridden for a day and a half before sighting him. The tracks they had followed showed Logan had ridden back and forth over a lot of Block W, around the pastures where the herds were; sign on a grassy bench showed where he had stretched out, watching men at work, branding, castrating, busting broncs and performing all the other chores a big ranch required to keep it running smoothly.

Rio had cursed, still stiff and sore:

the riding didn't do anything to ease the pain of his injuries and kept him in an aggravated state. 'Sonuver's been close to the house, too! Judas, he moves like an Injun!'

The two men he had with him were Pike — not his real name, not the one that was on several Wanted dodgers in other States — and the man they called 'Rowdy', simply because he rarely spoke. Taciturn, tough, good workers, both were willing to do anything for a dollar.

Now they had actually caught up with Logan and Rio unshipped his rifle. The hardcases glanced at one another.

Pike, rawboned and hungry-looking, said, 'Thought Tate said — '

'I *know* what Tate said, damnit!' snapped Rio, levering a shell into the breech. 'You two get down there, close by in those trees where he's waterin' his horse. Wave that red neckerchief of yours, Rowdy, when you're in position.'

'What you gonna do?' Pike insisted.

'I'm gonna make sure you need a

heap of dental work you don't do what I tell you! Now!'

They moved off, Pike shrugging. You couldn't tell what Rowdy was thinking: his face hardly ever changed from its set, rugged lines.

Rio grew impatient, lying prone now, watching Logan fill his canteen at the shallow stream down there, but he needed the other two close before he — Ah! There was the flash of the red neckerchief. He could just make out Pike and Rowdy but they were screened from Logan as the man stood up beside his horse, slapping the stopper into his canteen.

Rio lifted the rifle, sighted, and shot the sorrel through the head. The animal shrieked briefly, jumped, and crashed on to its side, kicking its last.

Logan dropped the canteen, sixgun coming out of leather as he crouched, looked for cover. He ran towards the barely moving horse. Rio put a shot into the ground in front of him and Logan dodged but tripped and rolled into the stream.

When he stood up, dripping, Pike and Rowdy had come into the clearing, mounted, rifles pointing at him. He stared a moment, rammed the Colt back into the wet holster and slowly lifted his hands shoulder-high.

'I've seen you two working on Block W.' Neither man had been there seven years ago.

They said nothing and Logan heard another horse picking its way downslope through the timber. He was mildly surprised to see the battered Rio walk his horse into the clearing: he began to see what was going to happen.

'When I didn't see you working around the spread, I figured you were still laid up in your bunk.'

'You'll wish I was.' Rio jerked the rifle and the other two dismounted after sliding their weapons into the saddle scabbards.

Logan narrowed his eyes as they moved towards him, closing in from either side.

'I know you're fast, Logan! But you so much as twitch and I'll blow your kneecap off!' Rio lowered the rifle barrel slightly. Then Pike and Rowdy reached for Logan's arms. He slapped their hands aside and hooked an elbow into Rowdy's neck, crushing his ear. The man grunted aloud in pain — the first audible sound Pike and Rio had heard from him in days.

Pike jumped back, dodging Logan's swing, stepped quickly aside and hooked a blow into Logan's midriff. Logan staggered, gasping for breath, then they had him in their grip and Rowdy punched him three times, very fast, in the face and side of the head. Rowdy's ear looked hot and red.

Dazed, Logan struggled but these were tough men, strong from ranch work and years of roughing it outdoors. Rowdy dragged the Colt from Logan's holster and tossed it into some bushes. By then Rio had dismounted and limped stiffly across, still holding his rifle.

He looked into Logan's cold eyes and, despite himself, felt his stomach leap. He had the same impression Tate had had when Logan had first appeared at the ranch gallery: that the man was looking at him down the barrel of a gun pointed right between his eyes.

Then he twisted his mouth and rammed the rifle barrel savagely into Logan's midriff. The man doubled as far as Pike and Rowdy let him, breath rasping, grimacing. Rio brought up the butt of the gun, bouncing it off Logan's head, making his hat fly into the stream, where it began to drift on the slow current. Blood trickled down his face and Rio smiled: that was what he wanted to see . . . Logan bleeding!

He used the butt and the rifle barrel to maul Logan, once even brought a muted curse from Rowdy when the front sight cut his hand as it slammed across Logan's ribs. The hardcases were supporting Logan now, his legs having given way.

'Hell, he's heavy!' gritted Pike.

They bared their teeth as Rio continued to enjoy himself. He dropped his rifle at one stage and pummelled with his fists, shouting an obscenity when he used his injured left hand inadvertently, the blow partly dislodging the bandage. Maddened by the pain, Rio used elbows and boots as Logan was released and sprawled face down. Rio crouched over him, kicked him twice in the body and then stood, swaying, sweat dripping from him, gasping for breath.

'If — if he hadn't throwed me down them — steps . . . ' he panted, 'I'd've . . . '

'You'd've likely killed him,' growled Pike. 'He's a mess as it is.'

'He'll know why. One thing, he ain't dumb.'

'He is if he don't quit this county after that beatin'.'

'He comes back or sticks around Tate'll give the word to — shoot him on — sight.'

Pike looked at him sharply. 'Reckon

he'll put a bounty on him?'

The words even had Rowdy interested in Rio's reply.

The ramrod nodded slowly. 'Reckon so. Come on, let's get outta here. We'll dump him off Block W land so's he'll be sure to get the message when he comes round.'

Pike grinned, then Rowdy surprised them both by speaking.

'Dump him to hell 'n' gone, in the roughest country we can find.'

They stared at the usually silent man, then Rio laughed and Pike took off his hat and made an exaggerated bow to his sidekick.

'Rowdy,' said Rio, still chuckling. 'Often wondered what goes on that head of yours. Now I know! You got plenty of good ideas, just don't talk about 'em.'

Rowdy managed a small smile.

'Yeah!' Pike agreed. 'Logan'll be lost, thirsty, hungry and afoot — in *Wilde country*! Get it? Wouldn't wish that on my worst enemy.'

‘The hell you wouldn’t!’ observed Rio. ‘Ah, well. Maybe I would at that!’

* * *

It was well into the afternoon before Logan stirred. He wasn’t aware of his surroundings or the sky or the hot sun blasting down on him. Though when he groaned and rolled on to his back, and he was face up, he screwed up his bruised eyes, even though they were already tightly shut.

It was the best part of another hour before he began to sort out his reluctantly returning senses. Pain was the first sensation, so much of it that he couldn’t pinpoint it: his entire body was one huge throbbing agony.

He vaguely remembered half-waking once before, when the sun had been at a different angle. Before noon, most likely. The pain and stiffness were going to be with him for a long time, he figured, still lying there, unmoving now.

Rio, Pike, Rowdy. He repeated the

names over and over in his mind: he knew he wouldn't forget them. In time he found out that he had no sixgun and there was no sign of his horse. Or the creek. He was no longer in the deep canyon where the trio had found him and killed the sorrel.

He didn't know where the hell he was!

The knowledge made him sit up. He started quickly enough but slowed almost at once, grunting aloud as new pain flooded through him from scalp to toenails. The world tilted and spun and even the sky darkened for a time.

When he was aware again, he was half-sitting, propped up with one hand pushed into the gravel, arm stiff. The other arm was sore and swollen from the beating.

Time passed and he found himself in amongst the heavy brush. The sun was slanting towards the west and he was hungry. And thirsty. Birds wheeled and screeched above but they were high up, not sweeping in towards their evening water supply. It must still be a long way off.

There was no use trying to figure out where he was: his vision wasn't stable. The whole scene kept going in and out of focus. He drifted into a half world and each time he clawed his way back, there was fresh pain — or an increase in what he was already suffering. Once he thought he heard cattle lowing. Another time he was sure he felt rain on his face but when his tongue darted out to lick it, there was a salty taste and he knew it was only sweat.

Soon after he began to shake and feel cold. He knew what that was: utter fatigue and even, possibly, the onset of fever.

Whatever it was, it overwhelmed him and halfway through a thought about trying to find some high ground so he could get a better idea of where he was, he fell into exhausted sleep.

* * *

Val Guthrie hadn't meant to ride so far. She was a long way from her ranch house. It would be dark before she rode into her yard tonight. The sun seemed to be falling almost visibly towards the mountain range.

She had been looking for a small box canyon, preferably one with good grass and water, though she could hedge on both of these if need be. Val was preparing for a maverick round-up and thought that if there was a halfway house in the ranges where her crew could leave the day's gather, it would save a lot of time, instead of having to drive them back to the ranch and then return to the ranges.

A couple of night camps wouldn't bother any of them. It certainly wouldn't trouble her: she had been an outdoors girl for most of her life and liked nothing better than sleeping under the stars, or a tree if it was raining and the stars weren't even visible.

So far she hadn't had any luck. There

were numerous box canyons or those with narrow entrances and exits that could easily be blocked with a sapling fence, but they all had some disqualifying feature: no water, or even too much — soggy ground that could bog restless cattle, short grass, or sometimes, horse belly-high, grass that could, and did, house numerous snakes.

This was unfamiliar country. Normally, she would not ride out this far, but last year's flood had driven a lot of the wild or unbranded cattle into the high country and many had stayed there. If she could find a suitable canyon up here it would be closer to where she hoped to round up a goodly number of mavericks, and increase her depleted herds.

Now, the light fading, she felt uncomfortable in this uninhabited area. She told herself not to be so foolish but when she caught a glimpse of the creek as sunlight reflected from it, she turned her mount that way instantly and forced a path through the brush.

The shadows were heavier and darker by the time she came out on to flat land with mostly bare low hills on either side of the lazy creek flowing through it. Looking around for familiar landmarks, she decided she must be to the north of her ranch and the Block W.

She certainly didn't want to run into any of Tate's riders with darkness falling rapidly. The horse was blowing from working its way through the thick brush and she walked it to the water's edge, dismounted, and knelt to drink a couple of yards upstream from where the horse was slaking its thirst. Not wanting the animal to drink too much when it was so heated, she struggled to pull it back before it bloated its belly. It was hard work but she managed to loop the reins over a stout branch of a bush and, wiping sweat from her face, went back to the water's edge to soak a bandanna. Moving her head this way and that as she ran the cool cloth over her face and neck, she suddenly stopped.

There were some old branches and a couple of saplings washed up on some rocks a few feet out. Something was caught on one of the slimy twigs.

Even in the fast-fading light she could see it was a man's hat. No cowboy she knew of would allow his hat to drift away without some effort to save it. Hats were almost sacred to cattlemen: first thing they put on in the morning, last thing they took off at night, although some slept with their hats merely tilted forward over their faces.

She waded out, stretched a little and almost lost her balance, but managed to grab the brim of the hat. It was dark and floppy and she knew it had been in the water for some time.

She looked inside. There was no name on the band but inked into the felt she thought she could make out an M and a 7 — no ranch of that brand around here. But turning it curiously, she saw it was really LW. It was not unusual for some men to put their name or at least their mark on their hats. If the ranch that employed the rider supplied the hat — it occasionally happened — then it would certainly have its name or brand marked inside the crown. But there were only the faded initials on this shapeless, waterlogged felt which could identify its owner.

Then she noticed the hole in the crown, frowned, and poked a finger through the sodden felt.

No doubt about it — it was a bullet hole.

Suddenly, a slight shiver ran through her as she realized she was the one who had put it there when she had found Logan Wilde camped on her land. Together with the initials, this had to be Logan's hat.

But — where was he?

6

Gone for Good

This time he *really* didn't know where the hell he was. That other time he could at least surmise he was still in the mountains somewhere outside the boundaries of Block W.

But *here*! How could he even begin to guess?

It was very dim for a start, although there were cracks here and there that showed daylight outside. He moaned involuntarily as he tried to move. Pain and stiffness made him stop the effort, pronto.

His mind was in a whirl; he felt as if he was on the lip of a precipice, swaying, always towards the yawning drop in front of him. His hands tightened and he felt saplings and rough gunnysacking, which made it a crude bed of some sort. The place smelled musty and there was stale smoke, not from a cooking fire but more like that of a forge.

That was a lucid thought, but it eluded him promptly and he felt the dizziness sweep over him. Just before he passed out again he thought he knew where he was: this had to be Ketchum's shack!

The knowledge made him try to sit up but it was too much and he sagged back, gripped the sapling bedframe tightly, holding on as if he was about to fall off . . .

That son of a bitch!

Zack Ketchum, mean, dirty and miserable. Lived alone in a shack in the mountains behind Cedar Butte and hit town once in a while with a little gold dust, enough for a spree that usually ended with him spending at least one night in the sheriff's cells.

Then he had hit paydirt and came to town ready to paint it every colour of the rainbow. Ketchum surprised everyone by using the bath-house and buying new clothes. Haircut and a shave and he was barely recognizable as the cantankerous semi-outcast prospector from up in the hills, who loved to drink and brawl, whore around and gamble.

He was amazingly generous with his money from the gold, bought drinks for the bar several times, even shared a couple of 'fallen doves' with drinking cronies. No cell bunk for Ketchum this time: it was the best room in the house at the Dearborn Hotel, but he was thrown out after making too much racket, damaging the furniture, and for bringing painted women from the nearby cathouse to his room for a party.

Still looking for a good time, Ketchum had decided he could afford to gamble a little — maybe a lot! He lost at keno, won a little at faro, finally, sat in on a poker-game.

Young Logan Wilde was one of the players, excited because he had built up a good-sized pot and wouldn't have to figure out ways of getting ready cash out of the Old Man for quite some time.

One by one the players tossed in their cards until it came down to Logan and Ketchum. The latter was red-eyed, soused from days and nights of debauchery, hadn't been properly sober since an hour after hitting town.

He realized with a shock that he had much less money left than he had reckoned on. A steamy anger raged through him and he started to swear aloud. *Must've been that last whore, rifled his pockets while he slept . . .*

'Your hand can't be that bad, Ketchum,' Logan said. 'You wouldn't've put so much into the pot if it was — and you're sure not much of a bluffer.'

'I can bluff you clear off the damn Block W, for all the Wilde money you can call on!' growled Ketchum, and a few onlookers moved away: they had seen Ketchum before when he was ready to turn nasty and they reckoned it was not far away now.

When, inevitably, he lost the hand, and accused Logan of cheating, Zack Ketchum jumped up, fumbling at the ancient Dragoon percussion pistol he carried in his belt. The worse for drink, unsteady, and blinded by the rage that swept through him, Ketchum was hopelessly slow.

He fumbled the Dragoon and dropped its four-pounds weight on to the edge of the table. He grabbed for it and upset the entire table, money and cards spilling to the floor. Logan had already drawn his pistol but held his fire: he had not earned a reputation of being a fast gun at this time.

When he saw his winnings scattered on the floor and some of the crowd grabbing what they could, he roared, fired a shot into the air, scattering the opportunists. Ketchum wasn't fazed, though, and swung up a chair, throwing it at Logan. Logan batted it aside, but a leg hit him above the right eye and split the flesh. Briefly stunned, he staggered back and Ketchum hit him again with the same chair and he went down, lights swirling in front of his eyes.

He came round sitting in another

chair, the barkeep, Larry, wiping his face with a wet cloth. It was bloody and, blinking, young Logan put a hand up above his eye, saw blood on his fingers, *remembering Ketchum then* . . .

Dazed, he lurched to his feet, looking around wildly. 'Where is he? Where's Ketchum?'

There was a small crowd but he addressed his question to Larry. 'Lit out, Logan. With most of your money.'

Logan swore, raked his angry stare around at the crowd. 'And you let him do it!'

'Hell, he had that Dragoon in his fist by then. It might be old, but it's still a damn cannon. No one wanted to risk a slug from that!'

'Is he still in town?'

Larry shook his head. 'Someone come in to see what all the shootin' was about and said he'd seen Zack goin' lickety-split over the bridge. Still ain't sure if he stole the hoss or not . . . '

Someone pushed through the crowd then and, checking his Colt, Logan saw it was Tate, with Rio by his side as usual. Tate was ramrod of the Block W at that time, Rio a top hand, some said a troubleshooter for Tate.

'You in another ruckus, little brother?' Tate asked, sounding pleased at the prospect. 'You know what Pa said if you got into one more scrape . . .'

Tate couldn't keep the grin off his face and Rio smiled crookedly.

'Hell with you, Tate! I've just lost a couple hundred bucks. When I find that Ketchum I'll kill the son of a bitch!'

'Oooo, he is riled, ain't he?' Rio said, chuckling. 'You better calm down, brother. Killing-talk don't go down too well. 'Specially with Pa.'

'And you'd be just the one to tell him, wouldn't you?' Logan picked up his hat, set it on his head gingerly and shouldered Tate aside. The elder Wilde cannoned into Rio and they fought to keep their balance. By the time they straightened, both angry, the batwings were swinging with a clatter behind Logan as he went out into the night.

It took him two days to find his way to Ketchum's place in the hills and when he got there the man was dead, lying on the earthen floor, blood still warm and sticky where it trickled from his slashed throat.

Then, as he knelt beside the dead prospector, something smashed into the back of Logan's head and he fell into oblivion, stretching out beside the body . . .

Wait a minute! This wasn't Ketchum's shack where he lay on the sapling bunk, trying to gather his senses. This was seven years away from that mountain cabin and the dead Ketchum. So, where the hell was he? And what had happened?

His head thundered but now he recalled the beating that Rio, Rowdy and Pike had given him, the onset of fever and — he had no idea how he had gotten here, or where 'here' was.

He could see better now in the half-light and he pushed the blanket off him. *Where the hell had that come from?* Cautiously he swung his legs over the side of the bunk. He sat there, gripping the edge, letting the world settle to an even keel before trying to make another move.

It was then that he found someone had strapped his ribs with rawhide and canvas. There was a large, spreading purple bruise on his midriff, which smelled of arnica and he saw the stains of iodine on some cuts on his arm and left hand.

Someone had doctored him.

Then a narrow plank door opened in one wall and he squinted as sunlight spilled in. He saw a man duck his head to look inside, a complete stranger, a black form against the light. 'Thought I heard you stirrin'. Stay put.'

Then the door closed and he heard a bolt slide across. What the hell . . . ?

But he was too weak yet to lunge for the door. He fell, sprawling, on the floor. He had managed to get to hands and knees when the door opened again. This time he recognized the newcomer: Val Guthrie.

'I guess the — fever must still be — with me,' he murmured, shaking his head and blinking. But she was no illusion. She came into the small space and he saw the man who had first looked in, standing outside.

'You'd better get back on the bed.' She turned her head and said, 'Lefty, lend a hand.'

Between them, Val and the cowboy got Logan on to the sapling bed and he lay back gratefully, breathing hard, fighting to keep a clear head.

'You're on my ranch, in the lean-to behind the blacksmith's shed. I thought it better if you were . . . out of the way, in case anyone came looking for you.'

He stared at her, letting her words sink in. 'How did I get here?'

'I found your hat in a creek, backtracked a little upstream and came across your sorrel. It had been shot through the head.'

'Rio.'

She arched her eyebrows and Lefty, a young, muscular cowboy said, 'That don't surprise me none. The kinda thing Rio would do.'

She had returned to her ranch that night and next morning, with Lefty and one of her other cowhands, Jace Fletcher, who was a good tracker, had gone back to where the dead horse lay. It took most of the day but they found Logan way back in the hills, delirious with fever and badly beaten.

'We brought you here.'

'How . . . long've I been here?'

'A day and a half. We've seen some of Tate's men riding our line but I don't believe any real search has taken place.' Val smiled thinly. 'That brother of yours had one of his men in the hills watching this place, though. We saw the sun reflected off his field glasses. We've been shoeing horses in preparation for the maverick round-up, so we could come to the forge quite often without arousing suspicion.'

'He still there?'

'No. I had a good look round,' Lefty said. 'Jace cut his sign, too, near the gulch that's a sort of boundary between us and Block W. He went back home, whoever he was.'

Logan nodded, looked at the girl. 'You're more hospitable than the last time we met.'

She shrugged. 'I know a little more about you now. In any case, I wouldn't leave any injured creature helpless in the wild.'

He smiled slowly. 'Well — thanks, anyway.'

* * *

'He's gone, Tate. Nothin' more to worry about.'

Tate Wilde looked coldly at Rio. 'I've had your assurances before, Rio, about certain things that didn't work out.'

Rio shook his head. 'No, he's gone. Lost, or fell over a cliff. The kinda country we dumped him in, and the way he was beat-up — you can forget about him, Tate.'

That was exactly what Tate would

like to do: forget his younger brother once and for all.

Seven years ago he had thought he was rid of Logan for ever. Half the town had heard him say he was going to kill Ketchum when he caught up with him. It had been an easy thing to arrange: Ketchum was dead drunk when they found him, but it had been hell's lousy luck that had brought the Old Man into that country just after Logan arrived.

Marshall had heard about Logan's latest scrape, of course, and had ridden to Ketchum's place to square up to the prospector — *still watching out for Logan, damnit!*

He'd found Logan, all right, sitting holding a bleeding head with Ketchum's corpse at his feet. Marshall Wilde was nobody's fool: one look at the lump and wound on the back of Logan's head and he believed his son's story.

'Someone settin' you up, boy. You are the most *aggravatin*' ranny for findin' trouble!'

'It finds me, Pa.'

Whether Marsh might have suspected Tate's hand in this — and Rio's, of course — no one ever knew. But he gave Logan all the money he had with him and told him to ride.

'South. Hit the Rio an' cross it and keep on goin'! Someone's set you up but no son of mine's gonna be railroaded into the penitentiary. Besides, you've caused me grey hairs enough. Now git — and don't come back. I don't ever want to see you again.'

That was what Tate wanted to hear, but he never knew for certain sure that it was the Old Man who had burned down the shack after Logan had gone, with Ketchum's body inside. When it was found amidst the smoking ashes no one could tell how the prospector had died. Most folk figured he had gotten drunk on rotgut whiskey and overturned a lamp, was too sodden with booze to get out in time.

Marsh told the family that Logan had gone to Mexico — for good. 'If he's got any sense at all, he'll never return here.'

His eyes hardened. 'Too many folk after his hide.'

He made no other explanation and Logan's name was never mentioned by him again.

Tate could still feel anger at the Old Man for interfering in his plan to have Logan blamed for Ketchum's murder and locked away, maybe even hanged. After Marshall Wilde had finished, no one — except the killer himself, and anyone who had helped him — knew that Ketchum had been murdered. And Old Man Wilde wasn't about to say anything.

It was his last favour to Logan and Tate decided he would have to settle for that.

For seven years he had.

'But why the hell couldn't he stay south of the Rio?' he gritted half-aloud. 'What kind of twisted fate brought him back here at this time!'

Rio frowned, looking closely at Tate. 'I told you, Tate. You can forget about Logan. He's gone for good. Anyone asks, say he went back to Mexico, 'cause there was nothin' here for him.'

But Tate was a worrier and had a lot on his mind right now.

'I've reached the point where I wish I'd listened to you when you wanted to kill him. But I'd damn well still want to see his body! Just to be sure.'

7

Los Gringos

After another day, Logan was moved up to Val's ranch house, at night.

He was feeling better and moving much more easily. She looked at him closely and said, 'You have good powers of recovery.'

'Lots of practice.'

She didn't smile. 'I don't know about you yet, Logan. You're a Wilde and I can't help wondering — '

'Why you bothered helping me?' he cut in. 'Well, neither can I. But I'm much obliged, Val.'

She frowned slightly at his use of her name but made no comment about it. 'I suppose it's foolish of me but I'm going to ask anyway: What were you doing down in Mexico?'

After giving her a long, steady look,

he shrugged. 'Lots of things. I wasn't there for the whole seven years. I came back to the States every now and then — when a job seemed worthwhile.'

He stopped abruptly and she knew he had made a slip.

'A 'job'? You mean you rode with *bandidos*.'

Logan took his time. 'They called us *Los Gringos mercenarios*. A few Americans, a couple of Mexicans, even a Dutchman one time. We just sort of gravitated together in the same area, found ourselves back-to-back fighting off bandit rabble one time and stayed together afterwards.'

'All men on the run?'

'Yeah, but not all running from the law: bad marriages, pregnant girls, political trouble, family squabbles.'

'That would be you, of course.'

He nodded, pensive. 'Looking back, it was my own fault. Pa took a shine to me, named me after a brother of his whom he said I resembled. Tate took after Ma, bossy, contriving to get her own way.

Not that I blamed her: Pa was a hard man. Anyway, I guess I took advantage of his being a mite softer with me than with Tate. I raised a lot of hell one way and another and he stood by me. I was pretty young when he banished me to Mexico. But he'd had a bellyful of me and my scrapes by then. He figured Tate would carry on the Wilde name.'

'You were afraid of him?' She lifted a hand quickly as he stiffened. 'I mean, you made no attempt to go back to Block W; did you?'

'I guess I was kind of scared of Pa. What happened was, we did some mercenary work down there; always some rebels wanting to change the *Presidente*, or a local *jefe* wanting to oust a rival. We got caught up in a fight at a place called Bella Mondo, and when it was over we found we'd hit a pay wagon. *Pesos* and gold.'

'The spoils of war.' There was a trace of contempt in her voice and she felt uncomfortable at the way he looked at her.

'Call it what you like, that money was ours — we'd earned it.' He paused to roll and light a cigarette, deliberately making her wait. 'As usual, there was trouble over the division of the spoils: gunplay when a few figured that a little killing would give them a bigger share. A bunch of them came after me, but I'd already lost the bag of money they thought I had, when I swam my horse across a flooded stream. They cut me off so that the only way left for me to ride was north — and the Rio was only a few miles in that direction.'

She waited but he smoked in silence. At last, impatience in her voice, she said, 'Obviously you escaped your pursuers.'

He nodded. The silence dragged on.

'Damn! You're an aggravating man, Logan Wilde!'

'I've heard it said. I crossed the border not far from Del Rio, which is not far from here. So I decided to try and make my peace with Pa. I like to think I'd gained a mite more sense than

I had before I went away.'

'I guess you knew that Block W was almost an empire too, and . . . ' She broke off when she saw the cold eyes hammering at her. 'What I mean is — '

'I know what you mean. No, I didn't want any part of Block W. But I didn't want the bad blood between me and Pa to continue, either. He was in his seventies and I figured it was time to bury the hatchet — if he wanted to.'

She flushed and looked slightly uncomfortable. 'I have a tendency to say exactly what I think.'

'I've noticed.'

She started to bristle, then relaxed some, even smiled a little. 'I'm surprised you didn't tell me to mind my own business.'

'Thought of it, but figured you had a right to know after what you've done for me.'

'Well, thank you for that. My tongue gets me into a lot of trouble at times.'

He had nothing to say about that, instead changed the subject. 'Why did

Pa want your land?'

'Because he saw it as a buffer between Block W and the sodbuster community that was setting up just over the range along the river.'

Logan frowned. 'I never saw any farms.'

'No. It never happened. Oh, it started with perhaps a dozen families, but we had floods and they suddenly realized why it was called 'river-bottom' land and the soil was so rich. It was washed away and some of the folk and their farms with it.'

'Tate give you a hard time?'

Val frowned and nodded slightly. 'Yes, he does, one way and another. Some of my men have been beaten up, a couple driven off. Fences have been torn down, pastures fired.'

Logan's mouth was grim. 'He wants you out of here.'

'That's obvious. 'Why' isn't. I'm no threat to a big spread like Block W. I don't run a tenth, even a twentieth, of the cattle Tate does.'

'But you don't really know Tate. He doesn't want your land as such. He just wants you off it because you made the whole of Block W look bad, beating them by filing on this land just when they had their eye on it. Pa wouldn't've ever forget that, and Tate won't, either.'

'But that's — that's ridiculous! You're saying he wants to ruin me, drive me off, and probably won't even use my land when he's done so? He just wants to prove Block W is all-powerful and when he goes after something, he doesn't give up until he gets it?'

Logan nodded as he exhaled smoke. 'That's Tate, and it's exactly what Pa would want him to do. Think back to when Pa was alive. You were still harried, I'll bet.'

Her frown deepened. 'My God, I was! Nothing I could really put my finger on or complain about to the law. It was Sheriff Keene at that time. Cattle would 'stray' into rough country and it would take days to round them up again. A few found their way into a bog, after a fence that had just been repaired mysteriously collapsed. I suspected Block W, of course, but there didn't seem to be any reason for it and a few other ranchers had similar problems. So, not being very experienced, I just put it down to small mischiefs I simply had to put up with.'

Logan stood and peered out the window. 'Guess I'd better stay out of sight for the time being. I'll leave soon as I can. But I will need a horse — and a set of guns.'

'I found your rifle half-under the sorrel. It's scratched up but otherwise all right. I don't know anything about your sixgun, though.'

'Rowdy threw it into some bushes, as I recollect.'

'I can give you one, and a horse. But you can't think of leaving yet. You need to recover a lot more.'

He smiled ruefully. 'That's the way I feel, but I don't want to impose.'

'If you do, I'll tell you.'

'I believe it.'

‘That’s just the way I am.’

‘Stay with it. No use putting on a face when it ain’t the right one.’

She regarded him speculatively. ‘I’m not sure about you, Logan. My instincts tell me to be wary because you belong to the Wilde family, but you’re so — different from Tate. Young Luke is a likeable enough boy and while I don’t really know Annie, I feel sorry for her. Everyone knows Tate won’t allow her to marry Dan Dalton. Personally, I don’t believe he has the right to deny her.’

‘Sure he does. She’s not twenty-one yet and he’s head of the family. Took over from Old Marsh.’

‘And, of course, *he* wouldn’t allow your sister to marry a lawman, either!’

‘I dunno. He liked Annie well enough, but I always figured that Pa would reckon no man would ever be good enough for her. I know he aimed to send her to some ladies’ school back east when she got older, but I left before that happened.’

‘Oh, she was attending a school in

Baton Rouge, I think, but Tate brought her back.'

Logan stiffened. 'Tate pulled her out? Goddamn, he's an arrogant son of a — '

'Yes, I agree. He is an arrogant son of a bitch.'

If he was surprised at her swearing, he didn't show it. He seemed mighty thoughtful.

'Was thinking I might just ride on — after I looked up a couple of people.'

'Like Rio? Pike and Rowdy?'

He nodded briefly. 'I'll still look 'em up, but I'm gonna have to stick around. See Annie gets a better deal. Luke, too.'

'What about yourself?'

'Nothing about me. I'm not in Pa's will and I truly don't care. But I figure I've got obligations to Annie and Luke. They can't stand up to Tate.'

She went to a cupboard and brought out a bottle of whiskey, poured two glasses, handed him one, looking him straight in the face.

'You've earned this, and I — I believe

I might even change my mind about you.'

'That so?' He sipped the whiskey. 'Good liquor.'

'Mmmm. Yes, I've just realized that I've been quite unfair. A man doesn't necessarily have to carry the reputation associated with his name — good or bad.'

His face remained sober and he knew it was as close as she would ever come to an apology. His nod of acceptance was so slight she wasn't even sure she had seen it.

He lifted his glass with the remains of the whiskey.

'Let's drink to that.'

* * *

The next day Jace Fletcher rode back with Birch.

Val met them on the porch and Jace, holding a Colt on Birch, said, 'Found him prowlin' our line up near Squaw Creek.'

'What's happened to him?' Her voice sharpened when she realized that Birch's injuries were from fists. 'Did you do that, Jace?'

Fletcher shook his head. 'Found him that way.'

'What were you doing on my land?'

Birch licked his swollen, split lips. He seemed mighty nervous, one bruised eye almost shut, a cheek all puffed up and cut, an ear heavy with dark, dried blood. And he sat the saddle awkwardly, as if his whole body hurt.

'I — I was tryin' to make up my mind to ride in.'

Val frowned. Jace nudged Birch in the back and the man jerked, grimacing.

'You were sneakin' around. I seen your tracks. You been there a while.'

Birch nodded, looking miserable.

'Who did that to you?' Val Guthrie asked.

'Rio — who else?'

'I guess you're fired from Block W then. What did you do to upset Rio?'

‘Nothin’. Was Tate set him on me.’

Val and Fletcher exchanged a puzzled glance.

‘It was because I told the sheriff Splinter was gonna shoot Logan but Logan was faster. Hell, was he fast!’

‘Tate was riled because you backed Logan’s story of self-defence?’

‘Yeah. They beat up on Hollis, too, for the same thing but he cleared out soon’s he could ride.’

‘And you came here. I’ve got no work for you, Birch.’

‘No, no. Not lookin’ for a job. Hell, sooner I quit this neck of the woods the better.’ Again he licked at his battered mouth. ‘I seen you bringin’ Logan down from the hills, just on dark the other night.’

‘He’s lyin’, Val! He’d have used info like that to save a beatin’.’

‘How about it, Birch?’

Birch shifted uneasily in his saddle. ‘I seen what they done to Hollis and knew I was for it, too. I — I did think I’d tell ’em about Logan but Rio come up behind me and kicked the back of my knee. Can hardly walk now, and he slammed me face first into a tree and — worked me over.'

Jace curled a lip. 'So you never had a chance to tell him about Logan!'

Birch shook his head. 'No. But I'd made up my mind by then I wasn't gonna tell 'em, anyway. Tate's scared of Logan for some reason; thinks he's gone now Rio and Pike and Rowdy beat up on him. But he ain't sure. I figured Logan might be able to make trouble for Tate — and that sonuver, Rio.'

'You're a brave man, Birch!' Jace allowed sardonically.

Birch was past insults by now. He only wanted whatever revenge he could arrange without danger to himself.

'Suppose Logan knew about this,' Val said slowly. 'What would you expect him to do?'

'I dunno. But if he's hidin' here, it means he ain't gonna clear out and that means he'll square things with Tate and Rio some way. That's good enough for me.'

Val stared hard at him and Birch dropped his gaze.

'There's something else, isn't there?'

'Mebbe. But I'll only tell Logan.'

'Don't fall for that, Val! Whole thing's a trick just to see if Logan's here. What'd they do, Birch? Threaten you with more beatin's unless you come here and spun your damn lies? Just to see if it brings Logan out?'

Birch looked fearful. 'Judas, *no*! Look, I'm on my way outta this damn country. I just want to square away with them snakes at Block W. I swear that's gospel!'

Val studied the man a little longer, said, 'I think you could do with a drink of decent whiskey, Birch. Don't dismount if it's too painful. I'll bring it out.'

Birch looked grateful but Jace frowned as Val went back into the house. When she returned, he understood: she brought Birch a glass with whiskey in it, all right, but just inside the door, in deep shadow, Logan stood, sixgun in hand.

'You wanted to see me, Birch?'

The Block W man was just downing the whiskey and Logan's voice startled him so that he sprayed half of it into the air. 'God*damn*! You scared me white!'

'What you got to tell me, Birch?' Logan moved the gun a little so that it caught some light along the barrel.

Birch glanced at the girl and Jace Fletcher. 'Well I figured what I gotta say might be worth somethin' to you.'

Jace made a disgusted sound and Logan said, 'No good, Birch. I'm about broke.'

'Tate wouldn't pay me what he owes me!'

'Hard luck. Now, either speak up or ride on out.'

'It's kinda . . . private.'

'Tell me anyway — and now!'

Still Birch hesitated, gave his attention to Val as if he hoped she might offer him money for his information.

'I gotta have some money to get away!'

She gave no sign and then his beefy

shoulders slumped.

'All right, damn you! I'll settle for knowin' you'll square with them sonuvers at Block W eventually.' His next words came with a rush, tumbling over one another. 'I seen Old Marsh's will — the original one. Your name was in a couple places. Dunno what he left you, but Tate was lyin' when he said you never even got a mention.'

8

Firing Line

Val Guthrie came back into her parlour where Logan sat, smoking and looking thoughtful.

'I gave Birch twenty dollars and Jace is seeing him over the range. I wouldn't trust him going through town with money in his pocket.'

Logan nodded distractedly. She sat down opposite him in a worn padded chair.

'D'you think his story's true?'

'Yeah. I think it could be.'

'But why would your father have an ordinary cowboy witness his will? Birch wasn't even a top hand in those days, by his own admission.'

'That's true. But he was likely one of the few ranch hands who could read and write — and sign their name rather than with an X or some other mark.'

Val nodded slowly. 'And he said he just happened to be in your father's office at the time he was writing his will. It's possible, I suppose, Logan, but I've never felt that Asa Birch was anyone I would trust.'

'No. Birch always has his eye out for an easy dollar. And he's got a mean streak. But he's been working at Block W for a long time. I was just a kid when he first signed on. Pa used him as a messenger at times because he could read and write and he was a damn good rider. I dunno what the arrangement was, but you can bet Birch was paid pretty good.'

'And now he's been beaten and fired, and he's short of money.' Val shook her head. 'All the more reason to be suspicious.'

Logan sighed, drew deeply on his cigarette. 'Yeah, but it sounded like gospel. He said the will was written all in capital letters. Pa could never handle running writing too well; his right hand got mangled years ago and ever since his writing's been almost illegible. He'd want something like his will to be quite clear, so no words could be mistaken for something else. I've seen him make out bills of sale the same way and for the same reason.'

'What about his signature?'

'Oh, he wrote that all right. No one would make out 'Marshall B. Wilde', but it was an obvious scrawl and he always finished with a flourish, a kind of tail on the last 'e' coming back part-way over the other names.'

'Easy to forge?'

Logan shook his head. 'Pretty damn untidy, but distinctive. I wonder if McGowan kept the original will?'

'Not likely, is it?'

Logan crushed out his cigarette in a glass ashtray, looking at the girl. 'He might. 'Specially if he's got some deal going with Tate.'

'You mean, if Tate reneged on the deal McGowan could threaten to make the original will public?'

'Something like that.'

'But is Ash McGowan dishonest?'

Logan gave a short laugh. 'He's been known to bend the law in his direction — almost always does, actually. Pa caught him out once or twice, but still used him to his advantage.'

'Enough to entrust him to execute his will?'

Logan frowned. 'I dunno about that. Tate and McGowan say that's the way it is but if Tate did a deal to have a fake will drawn up, it would be lucrative for McGowan, you can bet on that.'

'Like a share in Block W?'

'It would have to be something like that. He doesn't make a big deal about it, but McGowan owns most of this county already, and Block W is the biggest spread in Texas.'

They were silent for a time, each with their own thoughts, mulling over all the implications. Then Val said,

'Obviously you need to see the original will. If it still exists. The date of each will would be important.'

Logan nodded and began to build

another cigarette. 'I know where Pa kept the key to the ranch safe.'

She sat bolt upright in her chair, alarm on her face. 'You're not going back to the ranch!'

'No other way to check.'

'But Tate will never let you on Block W!'

'He don't have to know.'

'You're being foolish, Logan! You can't slip in there without being seen! His men probably have orders to shoot you on sight!'

'They won't even see me if they've got something else to keep them busy.'

'Oh, no. You're not using my men for whatever hare-brained scheme you're thinking up!'

He stood, a little stiffly, stretching cautiously.

'Not to mention you're not yet fit!'

'Fit enough.'

She started to protest further but when he drew his Colt and began checking the loads, she saw it would be a waste of time.

* * *

He gave the ranch hands time to turn in so that he would only have the nighthawks guarding the main herd to worry about.

A shadow moving through the blackness, he checked and found there were four riders, each having their own section of the pasture to watch. If he knew nighthawks, they would meet up and share cigarettes and gossip once the herd settled down. It was a quiet night, a little scud sliding across the stars, and only a nascent moon, just starting to rise over the hills.

The pasture he chose was one that was a winter holding-paddock, surrounded by brush, including a patch of sotol, noted for its flammability. And there was good grass growing there, ready to receive cattle after early winter round-up. It was not only a valuable asset to have on call, but it was a long way from the river: *that* was important now.

Lefty, the big young cowboy who had been with Val when they had found him in the rough country, was a cheroot smoker. He reluctantly gave Logan four from his packet.

'You better buy me a new lot.'

Logan promised he would and now took the cheroots from his shirt pocket. He crouched down in a hollow and lit them one by one, drawing on each to make sure the tobacco was burning properly. The smoke was too strong for his taste and he had to smother a cough.

Still crouching, he took off his hat, held the cheroots in one hand inside the crown and moved into the pasture. The sotol patch was the first place he stopped and used two of the cheroots, drawing on them first before planting them in small mounds of dried leaves and grass which he had gathered and placed under the bush.

He had to take a chance here and go up out of the hollow to place the other two cheroots where he wanted them.

One of the nighthawks was singing some mournful ditty as he let his mount walk slowly around his section of herd. No one had seen Logan placing his improvized fuses.

He went back to where he had left his horse, a high-shouldered grey Val had given him to use. He had made sure it was a gelding: he didn't want a stallion that might start trumpeting when he smelled the remuda mares on Block W.

On foot, he led it away from the pasture and was well on his way to the ranch house, moving through trees beyond the yard behind it, when the first flames started as the cheroots burned down into the dry grass and leaves.

Within a couple of minutes three fires were burning, the sotol patch beginning to roar as flames writhed high.

The nighthawks had seen them now and were shouting, riding in on the pasture. They dismounted, started beating at the fires with green branches ripped off nearby trees, one man using a saddle blanket.

It was no use; the fire had taken too big a hold and moments later one of the nighthawks was riding hell for leather to the ranch house.

Logan stayed put and watched the panic take hold. The rider fired his sixgun into the air, shouting to arouse the sleeping cowhands. Men came pouring out of the bunkhouse, some half-dressed, a couple completely naked. The ranch house door was wrenched open and he knew it was Tate, shouting and giving wild orders once he saw the fires.

The countryside was lit up by the leaping flames and the bushes crackled as they were incinerated, sounding like a remote gun-battle. Horses were racing to the pasture. So was a buckboard loaded with sacking; this would be wetted in the distant river, probably, and used to beat at the flames. And plenty of wooden pails were being carried along so a bucket-brigade could be formed.

'Goddammit!' Tate bawled. '*Move*, you lazy sons of bitches! Wake up! Save that winter feed, for Chris'sakes.'

At an upstairs window in the big house, Logan recognized Annie looking out curiously. Luke was likely out with the men lending a hand.

He moved around more to the back, ground-hitched the grey and made his way to the house. The office window was on one side and, as usual, the window wasn't locked. The catch had given trouble for as long as he could remember and had never been fixed. It was one of those piddling little awkward jobs that were always going to be done 'when we're not busy'.

The frame was warped a little and jammed not quite halfway up, but rather than risk making a lot of noise — the house cook and other servants would still be in their rooms, he guessed — he managed to worm his way inside.

He groped his way around, banged into the desk unexpectedly and cursed Tate for changing the furniture around. But he found the door and turned the key in the lock. He kicked a floor rug along the bottom so no light would show under the crack and struck a match.

The battered old bookcase was still there, stuffed with copies of *Cattlemen's Journal*, and tattered *Harper's Weekly* as well as a few issues of the local Cedar Butte *Clarion*. It was heavy but he moved it a few inches out from the wall, his muscles cracking. He felt a couple of half-healed cuts break open on his arms and back. Groping, scraping his forearms on the back of the bookcase, he felt the nail head where Old Marsh had always hung the safe key.

It was empty: the key was no longer kept there.

Logan swore softly. *Now* where the hell would Tate keep it? It was pointless to speculate: he would have to search. Distant shouts and cries could still be heard from the burning pasture and the smell of smoke was strong.

The desk was the obvious place to

start but he would have to keep striking matches — or maybe he could risk lighting a lamp, keeping the wick turned low . . .

Then, all at once, it wasn't necessary. He found the key, old and worn as he remembered, lying under an untidy stack of papers in the bottom drawer.

He went to the old safe in the corner and had just slid the key into the brass-faced lock when a door he hadn't known about — obviously put in since he had left — opened and a man holding a sixgun stepped into the room.

'Who's there? I see you. Now don't move or I'll shoot!'

A light glowed behind the newcomer and as Logan stood slowly, hands lifting, he saw Annie holding a lamp.

'You both make fine targets,' Logan said quietly.

He heard Annie gasp. 'Logan? Is that you?'

'It's me, Annie. Who's your friend?'

'We've already met, Logan,' the man said quietly, and then Wilde saw the lamp light reflected from the brass star on the man's pocket.

'You're about the last man I expected to find here, Dalton.'

Annie came towards him. 'Oh, Logan! Don't . . . don't give us away. Please! Dan and I, well, we — '

'I ride out sometimes at night and give a signal that only we know,' Dalton cut in. 'It's risky, but it's the only way we can meet. Tate keeps Annie on too tight a rein so she can't slip away.'

'I guess you really do love her if you're willing to take such a chance.'

'Told you I do.'

Annie was holding to his arm now, and with a sudden realization, said, 'You set that pasture afire!'

'I need to see Pa's original will, Annie. It's either here or with McGowan.'

'McGowan has the will,' Dalton said. 'I've seen it.'

Logan tensed. 'I'm talking about the *original* — '

'There's only the one that I know about,' Dalton said.

'Written in ink, in capital letters?'

The sheriff frowned. 'The one I saw had been typed on that new-fangled writing machine McGowan's clerk uses.'

'Signed by the Old Man?'

Dalton hesitated. 'There was a signature over the printed name of Marshall Wilde. I took McGowan's word it was your father's.'

'What did the will say?'

'Just what everyone knows. The Block W was left to Tate, with provision for Annie and Luke to have a small share each when they reach their majority.'

Annie tightened her grip on his arm. 'What is it, Logan?'

'The will's a fake. The original left some of the ranch to me, according to Asa Birch and he claims he witnessed Pa's signature.'

'Oh, yes, I remember that,' Annie said. 'I took Pa in a cup of coffee as Birch was writing. Pa seemed annoyed at the interruption, but that was normal enough. He was mighty bad-tempered as you know, Logan. Much worse after you'd left.'

'Just a minute,' Dalton said quickly. 'The will McGowan showed me had been witnessed by himself and Miss Harper.' He looked squarely at Logan. 'I think you and me have to see Ash McGowan.'

'Suits me . . . ' Logan snapped his head around as he heard horses racing into, the yard. 'Damn! They must've got the fire under control.'

'Dan! Quick, quick! You have to get out of here! If Tate finds you . . . ' Annie was panicking, her voice rising.

Heavy boots sounded on the porch. She almost dropped the lamp and Logan blew down the chimney, extinguishing it. He hurried her towards the narrow door by which she had entered.

'Go back to your room! I'll be in touch! Move, Annie.'

Dalton was already squirming his way out of the partly opened window, and as Annie, stifling a sob, closed the narrow door after her, Logan pushed the sheriff out and threw a leg over the sill.

He sprawled in the dirt. By then Dalton had run to the rear corner of the house. Then:

'Hey! Who the hell's that? Hey, you!'

One of the riders returning had spotted Dalton. The sheriff spun and brought up his sixgun, smashing it across the man's head. As he fell, Logan jumped over him.

'Where's your horse?'

Dalton pointed towards the dark line of trees. Then Logan ducked back round the corner of the house as two more men came running. One had his gun out and he shot at the lawman's dark shape as Dalton made a dash for the trees. He stumbled briefly, righted himself and lurched away. The second man bent over the unconscious ranny. 'Judas, Milt, what . . . ?'

Logan stepped out behind the man and clubbed him to the ground. The other man, crouching, was still shooting at the sheriff. He started to turn as Logan surged up and kicked him under the jaw. He leapt over the cowboy, hearing others yelling in the front yard now, coming in a wild-eyed group, out for blood. Twisting as he ran, Logan triggered three shots over their heads, causing them to scatter.

Then he was in the trees. Dalton was somewhere ahead and well over to the left. Logan found his way to his horse and as he swung into leather, heard Dalton spurring away.

He weaved the grey through the trees, wild shots and curses reaching his ears. Bullets zipped and clattered through branches but well off-target.

Later, he caught up with Dalton halfway up the range, the smell of wet smoke still heavy in the air.

'That's busted things wide open,' Logan said. 'If Tate figures out I was after a copy of the will — '

'He won't.'

Logan stopped speaking, then asked, 'Why not?'

'We separated pretty fast. Chances are they'll think it was only one man.'

'I was likely spotted.'

'Don't matter. We're about the same size, and I dropped my sheriff's star at the edge of the trees.'

'You what? Why'd you do that?'

'Tate'll think I was trying to see Annie. She's got enough sense to deny I got to see her but he'll figure it was just me. Far as he knows, and everyone else, you've left the county or are still lost in the ranges.'

Logan grinned. 'Like I said once before, you seem OK to me, Dalton!'

9

Bounty

Annie Wilde pulled the bedclothes up to her neck and tried to look sleepy as Tate stormed into the room. He was covered in ash and sweat and smelled of smoke.

'Did — did you put out the fire, Tate?' He stared, one hand still on the doorknob, not answering. Nervously, she asked, 'How did it start? And I thought I heard shooting. Or maybe I was only dreaming . . . ?'

He put his hand in his trouser-pocket and flung something on the bed. She sucked in a sharp breath and reached for the brass badge sheriff's with a shaking hand.

'Where — where did you get this? It looks like the one Daniel wears.'

'Funny thing, I had the same notion,

seeing as 'sheriff' is engraved on it!' He dropped on to the end of the bed, his reddened eyes making her cringe inwardly, though she tried to stay looking bewildered, only half-awake. 'Found it downstairs in the yard. Couple of my men were knocked out, one gunwhipped, other kicked in the head.'

'I . . . I don't understand all this, Tate! Gunshots, mysterious fires, men knocked out — and — and Daniel's badge!'

He reached out and snatched it from her hand. She made a grab but he was too quick for her, shook the badge in her face. 'You're a lousy actress, sis! Dalton was here to see you, wasn't he?'

'I . . . I don't know what you're talking about.'

She cried out more in alarm than hurt when he suddenly struck her across the face. Her lower lip trembled but she was determined not to cry, even though her eyes filled with tears.

'You're lying! Dalton was here! He was seen running from the house.'

He shook the badge again. 'He lost this so it's no use you lying any more!'

'All right!' she said, unable to hold back a sob. 'Daniel was here. He — we just talked — then there was the fire and he thought it best to leave while everyone was busy fighting it . . . '

Tate frowned. 'Then why didn't he go before we got the fire out?' Suddenly he stood, speaking halfaloud. 'Wait a minute! Pike was gunwhipped near the office and he said the window was partly open.'

He hurried from the room and Annie gave way to tears, covering her stinging face in her hands.

She knew now that it would be harder than ever for her and Dan Dalton to meet. Tate would see to that.

Pike, nursing his lumpy head where Logan's gun had struck him, came into the office, immediately leery when he saw Tate's face tight with anger. 'You wanted to see me?'

'The office window was open as far as it would go because it always jams.

But wide enough for a man to slide through?'

Pike frowned, but nodded. 'You figure someone was in there?'

'I know damn well they were! The key was in the safe lock!'

'What were they after? Money?' Then Pike knew and he pursed his lips. 'Oh-oh! The Old Man's will! Judas, did they get it?'

'No.' Tate's lips were drawn tightly across his teeth. 'I don't think they even got the safe open. But that fire was lit by someone who wanted us away from the house.'

'The sheriff? Just to spend a little time with Annie?'

Tate shook his head. 'I think there were two of them.'

'I only saw one.'

'But Chick said he was shooting at a man who looked like Dalton when he heard something behind him, half-turned and a boot caught him under the jaw! There were two of the sons of bitches!'

'Who else beside Dalton?'

'Who would be interested in seeing Pa's will? Yeah! Logan! Goddamnit, I knew he was still hanging around! I could feel him.'

'We-ell, I guess he coulda found his way out of that rough country. But he'd've been on foot, and where the hell would he hide out?'

'Someone's helping him, of course! Don't ask me who, because I have no idea. But he's likely still got a couple of friends from years ago who might go to bat for him.'

'Hell, we should've put a bullet in him like Rio wanted. But he said you didn't want him dead.'

'No. Thought it might look kind of suspicious. But by hell, I want him dead now! If he's working with Dalton . . . '

Pike whistled softly. 'I'll do it, Tate. You make it worth while.'

Tate Wilde glared at his employee. 'All right! It's worth two hundred bucks to me to see Logan dead.'

Pike smiled thinly. 'It's worth a

helluva lot more'n that! I'm not riskin' my neck goin' up agin him for a lousy two hundred.'

Tate was breathing heavily now, but he reined in his temper; he didn't care to be held up by one of his hardcases, but he knew he had to up the ante if he wanted results.

'All right. A thousand bucks on Logan's head. But not just for you, Pike. I'm bringing the whole crew in on this. I want him dead — and dead in a hurry!'

'Yeah, well, I'm gettin' outta here right now. Gimme a half-hour's start, Tate. You owe me that after all the stuff I've done for you.'

'All right. But go warn McGowan. Tell him Logan's after Pa's will and he'd better destroy the original he's got in his safe.' He grinned crookedly. 'Who knows? You might be lucky and find Logan there ahead of you. Then you can collect your thousand.'

Pike hurried out, trying to forget his throbbing head. He wanted that bounty but Logan was a tricky sonuver — and deadly.

On his way to the bunkhouse he decided to bring Rowdy in on it; at least he knew Rowdy would stay tight-lipped about the bounty.

And he was not squeamish about shooting a man in the back.

* * *

They were nearly back to town before Logan realized that Dalton had been hit.

He had noticed the man swaying a little in the saddle from time to time but up to now had put it down to weariness. Coming up on the other side of the lawman's mount, he saw the spreading dark patch on the man's trousers, about thigh level.

'Why the hell didn't you say you'd been hit?'

'Wasn't bothering me. But I think the lead's still in there. Giving me hell with every jolt now.'

'We better stop and I'll see what I can do.'

Dalton started to rein down. 'Just tie something around my leg to stop the bleeding. I'll go see Doc Hershey when we reach town.'

They dismounted and Logan knotted his own and Dalton's neckerchiefs together, tied them around the outside of the trousers. 'Bleeding pretty bad. Sooner we get you to the sawbones the better.'

He helped the sheriff back into the saddle, Dalton grunting a few times with the pain. 'Be kinda awkward for me, a lawman, having a brother-in-law if he's an outlaw.'

Logan smiled. 'Not this side of the Rio. I might stay for the wedding but I guess I'll be long gone by the time you're back from your honeymoon.'

Riding slowly now as they approached the darkened town, Dalton asked, 'What about Block W? I mean, if there's a will that leaves it to you . . . ?'

'I'll be surprised if there is, but it'll

probably be null and void if McGowan can produce a new one.'

'You'll let Tate take over then?'

They rode towards the bridge leading into Main before Logan answered.

'You may not have Tate for a brother-in-law, Dan.'

The sheriff started to rein down but Logan rode on ahead and he had to follow and direct him to the doctor's house. Logan remembered after Dalton named the street. They stopped outside the doctor's and Logan helped the sheriff dismount. As he did so, he looked at another house, four along and on the other side of the street.

'Miss Harper still live there?' He indicated the house with a climbing rose over the latticed entry to the porch.

'Not sure. I know she lives somewhere over this way.'

Doc Hershey, wearing a wrongly buttoned robe over his nightshirt, wasn't pleased to see them, but he grumpily led the way to his infirmary down a small hallway towards the back of the main house.

'Don't wake my wife,' he said in a hoarse whisper, as Logan steadied the sheriff on the edge of a narrow table and the medic untied the blood-soaked neckerchiefs. He was a middle-aged man, always looking tired, with bags under his eyes. He took down a pair of spectacles from a shelf and a clean cloth, mopped away the blood. Dalton sucked in a sharp breath through his teeth.

'I'll have to cut that bullet out. You've fibres and threads from those filthy trousers, too. I'm going to have to keep you a-bed for a couple of days until I make sure infection isn't going to set in.'

'I can't afford that much time away from my office!'

Doc Hershey merely raised his gaze to the lawman's pain-drawn face. 'Then don't. But when I have to decide whether to take your leg off to prevent the spread of gangrene, you may wish you'd listened to me.'

Dalton couldn't quite cover the alarm that drained the colour from his face, leaving him ashen. He glanced at Logan. 'I'd do as Doc says, Dan.'

Hershey snorted. 'Then you've certainly changed! You'd never listen to me after I patched you up from some of the brawls and other high-jinks you got up to seven years ago.'

Logan shrugged. 'I left that other feller down in Mexico, Doc. He wasn't as smart as he thought he was seven years ago.'

'Glad to hear it. Now scrub your hands and we'll get started.'

Logan stiffened. 'I've got things to do, Doc.'

'They can wait. If this foolish damn sheriff of ours loses much more blood he'll go into shock, and probably end up in Boot Hill.'

Logan sighed and started rolling up his sleeves. 'Where's the soap?'

'You'll need more than soap. That brown bottle with the ribs on it.

Carbolic Acid. Lather your hands with that after the soap — and don't take all night.'

Logan glanced at Dalton and was surprised to find that the man had passed out on the narrow table.

The bullet had hit Dalton as he was running away and had angled inwards, in a long line, going deep after lodging in the thigh muscle. Hershey remarked he didn't know how Dalton had ridden so far and fast and still stayed in the saddle.

It took a lot of probing and Hershey dosed the reluctant sheriff with several lots of laudanum to help reduce the intense pain. He was sleeping deeply by the time the doctor had stitched the large cut he had had to make, and bandaged the wound, leaving a thread at one end to drain it.

'He's not going to be happy when he awakens.' At Logan's puzzled look, he added, 'He won't be able to walk for a few days and then there'll be crutches for a short time.'

'Best tell his deputy then, Doc.'

'He doesn't have one — not a permanent one. Dan Dalton doesn't need one. He keeps the peace very well by himself, though he does hire temporary deputies on occasion, such as when a trail herd passes through to the railhead.'

Logan stifled a yawn. 'Best hope none come through while he's laid up. Well, if that's all, Doc, I'll be going.' He pulled the drapes aside a little and was startled to see it was almost daylight.

'You're welcome to spend a couple of hours on one of the empty beds.' Hershey gestured to the three empty iron-framed beds in the infirmary. 'You'll fall asleep in the saddle if you don't.'

Logan hesitated but agreed, chose one of the beds, removed his boots and hat and stretched out. He was breathing deeply and easily within seconds.

On the way out the doctor noticed that Logan was holding his sixgun down at his side.

'I don't think you've changed all that much, young feller,' he murmured, pulling the door closed behind him.

* * *

Mrs Hershey wouldn't hear of him leaving without breakfast the next morning and Logan reluctantly allowed her to bully him into staying for the meal. It was substantial: three fried eggs, a dozen strips of crispy bacon, corn-cakes and a thick slice of home-made rye bread. Plus three large cups of excellent coffee.

'Ma'am, as my father used to say after one of my mother's four-course suppers, 'I have had an elegant sufficiency', for which I thank you. Now I do have to be going.'

'Look in on the sheriff on your way out, Logan,' the doctor said. 'I've given him the bad news; you might make it a little more bearable if you can get him to see it's the only course for him.'

Logan didn't want to, but he went to

the infirmary and found Dalton sitting up in bed, left thigh heavily bandaged, and a glum look on his face.

'Damn sawbones says I've to stay a-bed for at least three days! Then use crutches!'

'You'll still have two legs if you do what he says.'

Dan Dalton frowned. 'Well. Damnit, Logan! What's this town gonna do without a proper lawman? Even for a short time.'

'Hire one of your temporary deputies.'

'Aw, they're OK for a night patrol or a weekend, but nothing else.' Then his face lit up. 'What about you? You need a job! It don't pay too well but it'll be a few bucks in your pocket.'

'Not me. I've never packed a lawman's badge and don't aim to start now.'

'You're the man for the job, Logan. You're going to stick around anyway until you get this thing about the will settled. You might be surprised how much easier it'll be to do that if you're backed by a deputy's badge.'

'Don't try to con me, Dalton!'

'Come on. You owe me, anyway. I was trying to divert Tate's men to give you a chance when I got shot.'

Logan arched his eyebrows. 'Funny. I figured it was t'other way about.'

Dalton shook his head vigorously. 'No, no. You're in my debt and you can square it by taking a deputy's badge; just till I get back on my feet. Literally!'

Logan glared. 'I'm not so sure you would make a good husband for Annie!'

'I sure wouldn't if I was a cripple, and I'll damn well be outta here tomorrow, hell or high water, if you don't take that badge! I mean it.'

Logan shook his head slowly. 'You son of a bitch,' he breathed, half-smiling.

10

Badge Toter

Logan's knuckles were sore from rapping on the front door before it was eventually opened and the woman stood there, holding a gown around her over her nightdress. Awkwardly, she was trying to work a pair of spectacles out of a case, at the same time squinting at him.

'Yes? Who is it?'

The sun was up, but barely, and Logan touched a hand to his hatbrim. 'Sorry to disturb you, Miss Harper.'

The glasses were on now and she leaned forward to peer at him. 'It's . . . Goodness me, what do you want at such an early hour, Logan Wilde?'

'Deputy Wilde, ma'am.'

'I don't understand.'

'Sheriff's been wounded. He deputized

me to keep an eye on the town until he's recovered. Doc Hershey witnessed the swearing-in.'

She didn't seem convinced, but hesitated to say so out loud. Frowning, she pushed a couple of strands of grey-streaked hair back off her face. 'Well, what do you want?'

'Could we go inside, maybe?'

'Certainly not!'

'All right. I want you to open up McGowan's office. You do it every morning, I'm told.'

Her jaw dropped. 'But never this early! I see no reason to comply with your request, Mr Wilde.'

Logan lifted his hat slightly and scratched at his head, his boot preventing her from closing the door. 'Well, ma'am, you don't and you'll need Ash McGowan — to represent you at the hearing.'

'Hearing?'

'When, as a duly sworn deputy, I charge you with obstructing the law. I sure don't want to, but . . . '

Her face was angry now and she twisted the cloth of the robe tightly. 'That's a despicable threat! I'm not even sure it's valid. I have no proof you are a lawman as you claim.'

'Well I wouldn't want you to lose your job just to prove you wrong.'

She tried to close the door but he didn't remove his foot and after giving him an exasperated look, she turned and went back into the house. 'I'll have to change!'

Logan amused himself by looking over the parlour beyond the door, noting the neatness, the exquisitely crocheted antimacassars on the backs of the armchairs, the handmade doilies under vases and ornaments on the small tables and the mantelpiece, framed pictures, mostly of older folk: probably her parents and relatives. He remembered hearing years ago that she kept tintypes of Ash McGowan in her bedroom. Everything here was neat and in its place. The room seemed mighty lonely to him, despite the framed pictures. Poor, frustrated old maid . . . he felt bad about being rough with her. And there was more to come . . . unavoidable.

They walked through the almost deserted streets in silence, but when they reached the foot of the outside stairway leading up to McGowan's rooms she said sharply:

'I would like to formally protest at your bullying me into doing this, *Deputy* Wilde! And I will see to it that Mr McGowan brings some form of legal action against you.'

'That's your right, ma'am.' He gestured to the stairway, touching her elbow to urge her up. 'No need to be nervous. I won't harm you.'

Stiff with indignation she opened the door and led the way into the reception area where she worked, placing her handbag precisely on a section of desk that was obviously kept cleared for this purpose. She removed the long pin from her black straw pillbox hat, placed it in a deep drawer and raised the blinds. Sitting in her chair, tight-lipped, she folded her arms across the lace of her bodice, defiantly.

Logan snatched up the keys she had laid on the desk. He locked the stairway door from this side, dangled the ring with its several keys. 'Which one is for the safe in McGowan's office?' He hadn't meant that to sound so rough!

She was frightened by his grim look and by his tone. 'There's very little money kept on the premises.'

'You know I'm not looking for money.'

She said nothing and he made her stand beside the safe where he could see her while he rifled through the papers on the shelves: land deeds, ranch mortgages, past and current civil actions, many receipts from rental properties, legal files in manila folders. It was a large safe, standing as high as his shoulders, and the shelves were deep. He straightened and looked at the nervous woman.

'Where's my father's file? The one

with his original will?'

'I — I have no idea. Why don't you ask your brother?'

'McGowan would keep the original as insurance after drawing up the new one for Tate. McGowan's likely already a silent partner in whatever swindle they've thought up between them. And you can bet it involves Block W.'

'I resent that! Mr McGowan is as honest as the day is long and — '

'I need to see Pa's will! Now!' He felt a twitch when he saw tears forming in the old eyes. 'Look, I'm truly sorry, Miss Harper. But you witnessed the new one, printed it on that writing machine, so you know darn well there was another one before it. And if Pa never wrote that second will, the first one will apply. I need it to make sure Annie and Luke get what's rightfully theirs.'

'You stand to gain, too!' She said a trifle nastily but broke off when she saw his face. She slumped into a chair, wrung her hands in her lap, tears running down her old face now. 'Oh, the hours of sleep I've lost over that cursed will! Mr McGowan said I should type it on the machine because your father wrote it on his deathbed and it was almost illegible. He copied it as best he could from your father's scrawl and I worked from that.'

'In other words, you copied what he wrote and you have no idea whether it was correct or not! When was this?'

'The day before your father died. Tate brought the new will in.'

'Do you remember the date on the original will?'

'Oh, yes. It was my fif — my birthday.' She actually blushed, adding, 'I think I've said enough, Logan Wilde!'

'Nowhere near enough, ma'am. We always got along pretty good, you and me — even if you didn't approve of my antics.'

'That I did not! You were allowed to run wild — they used to call you the 'Wild Wilde'.'

'Guess I did take advantage of Pa a mite.'

'You were a young devil and I disliked you intensely.' She looked suddenly pensive. 'But then, one day a girl named Wilma Dane stopped me in the street and asked if I could tell her what she should do with a bank draft for a hundred dollars she had received in the mail.'

Logan's face was set in wooden lines.

'She said you'd sent it, after hearing her mother had died and, as she was the eldest — *all of fifteen years old, for goodness' sake!* — she was left with the job of bringing up her siblings, three sisters and two brothers.'

She paused and after a while Logan shrugged. 'I used to ride with her older brother, Hank, before he was killed in a stampede. He saved me from drowning once.' Miss Harper nodded with a knowing look and Logan said curtly, 'But we're supposed to be talking about Pa's original will, not Wilma Dane!'

She smiled slightly, seeing his embarrassment. 'Yes. He left it in our safe-keeping for three years. It made any previous wills null and void. I admit I was very surprised to hear he had written new one.' She dabbed at her eyes, looked steadily at him. 'I know what you're going to ask next. I could hardly *not* know the contents, making copies for our records. If I remember correctly your father left the majority of Block W to you, the remainder to be divided equally between Tate, Annie and Luke. It was clearly implied that he wished you to manage the affairs of the young ones until they reached their majority. I — I think he had the idea that such an obligation might . . . tame you somewhat.'

'I'm surprised he left anything to me. That's why I didn't even argue when Tate told me I wasn't mentioned in the will.'

'You father risked a lot for you, if it's true he covered up that Ketchum business. And that was before he knew of Tate's troubles. Marshall really missed you, Logan. He always said you were so much like his younger brother, the one you were named for. It's why he allowed you so much . . . freedom, I suppose. I knew him well enough to feel certain he longed for you to return.'

'Not the impression I got. What 'trouble' did Tate get himself into?'

'He apparently needed money and sold some Block W cattle without your father's permission.' She paused and, wringing her hands again, said in a hushed voice, 'Mr McGowan managed to keep him out of jail. Oh, I oughtn't to be talking out of school but I've been worried about certain things in this office for a long time. I tried to ignore them by telling myself they simply weren't my business, that Mr McGowan was quite capable of handling everything.' She paused, hesitant about continuing.

'Tate was in some other trouble, too?'

She sighed and nodded. 'He had gambling debts.' As she spoke her gaze went to the open safe briefly. 'Your father refused to pay them, of course. And it was right after that that he drew up a new will, the one giving you the major share. You'd been in Mexico for four years by then.'

Logan suddenly said, 'These debts — who held the markers?' Again her gaze wandered involuntarily towards the safe. He strode across, picked up a bulldog clip holding a thick wad of papers that he had thought earlier were rent receipts. He glanced up and saw her tight face. 'Sure! McGowan! Dan Dalton told me Ash has an interest in that new saloon — The Aces High. Now I see how that 'new' will appeared out of nowhere! He used Tate's debts to force him into making a deal.'

'I . . . I know nothing about that!'

'No, they'd keep it just between the two of 'em. For a share of Block W, McGowan would set up a 'new' will, supposedly written by Pa on his deathbed. And that's mighty suspect in itself.'

She sighed and nodded agreement. 'Yes. I believe your father would've been quite incapable of writing, or even communicating in any way. Oh, you've no idea how I've worried about this, Logan! I didn't want to believe it of Ashley but . . . ' She dabbed rapidly at her eyes again.

Logan looked up from examining the papers in the clip. 'Tate could even have been set up by McGowan, using cardsharps to make sure he lost heavily.'

'Your father told me, after Tate stole cattle from him, that while you had caused him no end of worry with your scrapes, at least you were honest and faced up to the responsibility of your actions. It was Tate's dishonesty, I think, that hurt Marshall most.'

'Miss Harper, I have to see that original will.'

'I honestly don't know where it is, Logan.' She glanced at the cottage clock ticking away the minutes on the wall. 'Mr McGowan will be arriving soon.'

Logan hated to give up now but he didn't want to cause the woman any more distress. 'What about the new will? The one you printed up. How did they fake Pa's signature?'

She coloured again. 'By tracing it, I believe, from the original document. I felt the impression on the underside of the paper where the pencil had been used in the tracing. Then someone simply went over it with ink.'

'You've been a great help, ma'am. I'm sorry if I treated you roughly.'

She smiled wanly. 'I think I feel better for getting it off my chest. I should've done something about it long before this.'

'Can I leave you to tidy up the safe? It'll be better if McGowan doesn't find me here.'

'Yes, yes. You get along. I'll just say I had some work I wanted to get out of the way and came in early.'

He hesitated, feeling awkward at the sadness she couldn't quite conceal; she had finally admitted to herself that the Ashley McGowan she had admired for so long, had feet of clay. It couldn't have been easy for her.

He touched a hand to his hatbrim,

unlocked the outside door, and closed it after him as he stepped on to the landing.

Two guns roared down in the alley and he staggered back as bullets tore into the doorframe, showering him with splinters. Down on one knee, sixgun in hand now, Logan ducked back as the guns hammered again. The bullets missed, though they came close.

He saw the gunsmoke below, a small pall each side of the entrance of the alley that led to the stairs from the street. Then he saw a rifle barrel as one of the ambushers holstered his sixgun in favour of the Winchester.

Logan made a good target out here on the landing. He could duck back inside but figured he had endangered Miss Harper enough. He snapped two fast shots at the gunmen. Then, in a sudden, blurring movement, he leapt over the rear rail of the landing, snatching at the protruding floor timbers on the stair frame, dangled for a moment before he released his hold and dropped several feet to the ground.

The rifle was firing as he sprawled, rolling. He spun in behind a trash barrel, palming up his Colt again, as bullets chewed at the warped staves, one ricocheting from an iron retaining band. He crouched low, removed his hat and held it slightly up above the rim of the barrel on the end of his Colt.

A bullet chomped a shower of splinters from the top of the staves next to the hat. He saw where the man with the sixgun was hiding: in a corner where the building extended into the alley in a line with the other structures. Logan waited and when the man cautiously looked out to see what damage his shot had done, Logan fired. His bullet ripped a jagged, foot-long length of wood from the corner and the man there screamed as the splinter drove deeply into his side.

Rowdy had just made the biggest sound he would ever make this side of Hell. He staggered into the open, clawing at the protruding length of wood, hands bloody. Logan brought him down with another shot and Rowdy kicked his last in silence.

After hurriedly reloading, Logan watched the other side of the alley where the rifleman was. The man, apparently shocked by Rowdy's sudden and bloody demise, stepped out, rifle butt braced into his hip as he worked lever and trigger, raking Logan's position with the remaining bullets in the magazine.

Before the man ducked out on to Main, Logan had recognized him — without surprise: Pike.

He started running towards the alley mouth, glimpsing curious folk tentatively poking their noses in to see what all the shooting was about. A woman cried out and snatched a child out of the way as Logan pounded into the street. He couldn't see Pike, looked around at the folk who were hurriedly moving away from him.

'Where'd he go?'

One man, ushering his wife away,

turned to look over his shoulder and said, 'Down by the freight buildin'.'

Logan could see a faint haze of dust there now and pounded down Main itself, staying off the boardwalk where his thudding boots would warn of his approach.

Coming level with the laneway, he slowed, saw movement at the far end — no, *beyond* the lane's end. A man was running through weeds, leaping over a narrow muddy gutter from the town's drainage system, heading for the trees and scrub on the far side.

Logan snapped a shot, heard it whine off a sapling. Pike stumbled on a raised piece of ground, rolled on to his back and fired his sixgun: he must have dropped the empty rifle somewhere along the way. Logan dived to the ground, rolling in close against the last of the freight line's buildings. Pike's lead slammed into the wall four feet above him. When he looked up, Pike was weaving between the trees, crashing through the scrub and bushes. Logan pounded after him, leapt across the muddy drain, stumbled, got his legs under him again and smashed his way into the brush.

Pike must have used the noise of his progress to get his position, for lead whined past his head and he instinctively flung himself behind another bush. But he didn't delay, rolled quickly, bounded up behind a sapling about half as thick as his body. Bark and sap exploded right in front of his face and he clawed at his eyes, staggering enough to reveal himself.

Pike stepped out ahead, lining up his smoking Colt, in both hands, aiming steadily, a tight grin on his grimy face. 'Thanks for the thousand bucks, Logan!' he panted and fired.

Logan spun away, dropped out of sight behind a low bush. Warily, eager to see if he really had qualified to claim the bounty Tate had put on his brother, Pike sidled in, hammer cocked, trigger depressed.

Then Logan rose seemingly out of

the ground only a few feet away, his Colt blasting in three rapid shots. Pike was hurled back, arms flying out to the side, his gun going off, recoil kicking it from his grip. His head crashed violently into a tree and he rebounded, mouth open and gushing blood as he tumbled to the ground.

Logan still had one cartridge in his cylinder and he thumbed back the hammer, keeping the hot Colt barrel levelled as he approached Pike's bloody form, ready to shoot if the man was only shamming.

He needn't have bothered.

* * *

'Hell almighty, man! You've only been a deputy for a couple of hours and there're two men dead already! The folk in this town ain't used to running gun battles in the streets!'

Logan looked calmly at the irate sheriff sitting up in his bed in the infirmary. 'I guess Pike and Rowdy didn't know that.'

Dan Dalton glared. 'They do now!'

'They were hoping to collect a thousand bucks.' The sheriff frowned, not understanding. 'Someone's put a bounty out on me.'

Dalton pursed his lips, seemed to hesitate slightly before he said, 'Tate?'

'Looks that way.'

'Does he hate you that much?'

'We never did get on too well. He used to beat me up till I started to fill out and grow.'

'Then it was his turn to take a hiding, huh?'

Logan shrugged, turned as the doctor entered and, despite Dalton's protests, gave him some kind of medicinal draught.

'That'll ease the pain, though it won't help the wound's healing.' Hershey turned his gaze on to Logan. 'Getting like old times, but I don't really need the business, Logan. Enough folk die here of natural causes to keep me busy.'

Doc Hershey was also the town undertaker.

'Don't aim to make a habit of it, Doc. Listen, could Pa have written a new will the day before he died?'

Hershey reared back. 'Don't be ridiculous! He had full-blown tetanus. Violent and painful reaction to loud noises, must have suffered terrible agony throughout his entire body. Victims sometimes go into muscular spasms that can arch the spine like a bow — snap it completely. It's a horrible way to die and no one would have the slightest interest in — or awareness of — anything else but getting the dying over and done with.'

The medic broke off when he saw how tight and pale Logan's face was.

'Oh, good God! Forgive me, Logan! I didn't mean to be so — graphic. But it is such an impossibility that Marsh could have written anything at that time. He was long past communication of any kind.'

'It's all right, Doc. I never did figure the Old Man would go out peacefully, but I thought mostly of a riding accident or something out on the range, not this — lockjaw.'

'It was a rusty nail, from floorboards in an old part of the stables. The tetanus bacillus thrives in moisture and muck like that. I'm afraid he never had a chance, there's no known cure.'

Dalton said, slowly, 'I guess you know for sure now your father never wrote that will that gives Tate control of Block W.'

Logan nodded. 'Now all I've got to do is find the original.'

'If they haven't destroyed it.'

'I don't think so. I reckon it would be kept, as a threat to keep Tate in line. If he doesn't do as he's told, McGowan will suddenly find something wrong with the 'new' will and the original will surface and destroy Tate's plans.'

The doctor asked shrewdly, 'Would it benefit you if it did surface, Logan?'

'I'm not interested, Doc, but I'd sure like to make it better for Annie and Luke.'

Dalton squirmed a little on the bed.

'Can you keep an eye on Annie? Make sure she's all right?'

'I can try. But Pike and Rowdy might not be the only ones interested in that bounty.'

Dalton nodded slowly. 'Go to my office and pick up a deputy's badge. Wear it. They might think twice about killing a lawman.'

Logan stepped to the window and peered out.

'What're you looking at?' Dalton asked.

'Just wondered if any pigs happened to be flying by.'

11

Deputies Die, Too

'You should've sent someone with brains to do the job, not a couple of dumb-clucks like Pike and Rowdy. They'd be lucky to take the right calibre bullets.'

Tate Wilde glared at Rio across the ranch office. 'You mean I should've sent you!'

Rio shrugged. 'Logan'd be dead now.'

Tate continued to glare, then nodded slightly. 'Dalton's deputized him. Makes it that much harder.'

'Why? Deputies die, too.'

'Christ, man! He's officially the law now! McGowan is leery of him for the same reason. He checked up to make sure it was all done legal and with Doc Hershey as witness . . . ' He shrugged. 'Logan's the law here till Dalton gets on his feet. Like it or not.'

'Tate, Logan's the law, OK, but only as long as he's alive.'

Tate looked uncomfortable, toyed with a stone ink-bottle on his desk. Then his face hardened. 'All right. I'm between a rock and a hard place. McGowan's made sure Logan can't legally claim a share of Block W, but *I* haven't got it, either! Oh, far as anyone knows I'm running things, but Ash McGowan is in the background, already cutting himself a slice — and I know damn well it's gonna get bigger and bigger 'til he's got the lot.'

Rio spread his hands. 'OK. Put the thousand-buck bounty on McGowan. I'll collect within twenty-four hours.'

Tate's fingers rapped the desk edge, his gaze on Rio. 'Don't tempt me.'

'Hell! Do it! I can use a thousand bucks.'

'It's not that simple. McGowan's holding Pa's original will. If I don't go along with what he wants, or anything happens to him, he'll bring it out into the open.'

'Why? He wouldn't get a share at all then.'

'Well, that's the way it looks, but McGowan's no loser. He'll have something up his sleeve. No, nothing'd better happen to him.'

Rio sighed, showing his exasperation. 'OK, then somethin's gotta happen to Logan. Then it won't matter if McGowan comes up with the earlier will or not, because Logan won't be around to claim his legacy.'

The rancher scrubbed a hand down over his face. 'I'll have to think about it, Rio.'

Rio stood up. 'Longer you delay, the harder it's gonna get. You said you want me to pick up the mail when I go into town for those new fencin' tools. How about I stay over, come back tomorrow mornin'? The holes and posts won't be ready till then, anyway.'

Tate was suspicious but growled his permission. It might be that Rio only wanted a woman or a few drinks, but more likely he had something else in mind; the man had that look about him that Tate had seen a hundred times before.

He had some devilment planned.

The knowledge did nothing to improve Tate's mood.

* * *

Luke had had a bellyful of dirty, menial jobs. It seemed that every filthy corner of the ranch needed cleaning out and it always fell to him to do it.

He had argued with Tate about it before but there was something about Tate that scared him. It wasn't anything he could name or put his finger on, but — well, maybe it simply came down to a *look* in Tate's eyes.

It wasn't always there but when it was, Luke felt himself go cold, as if the winter winds had caught him wet and naked. He actually felt goosebumps creep across his skin.

He decided one night, lying awake in his bed, locked in his room as usual, that the strange, scary look was uncaring: that Tate didn't give a damn about him or anything else except his own desires when that particular mood was upon him.

But this was the last straw: cleaning out the pig pen after the biggest sow in this part of Texas had given birth to a litter of twelve. Ten now, for two had been smothered trying to reach her teats. But the place was covered in excreta and afterbirth as well as the usual slush.

Luke had slipped and landed in a filthy puddle. He now smelled like a cesspool in midsummer. He was standing there, trying to scrape some of the muck off his trousers, when he heard someone laugh.

He rounded swiftly but had already recognized that mocking laughter; big brother Tate, highly amused at Luke's discomfort, was leaning on the fence rail.

'Bet every time we have bacon for breakfast you'll wish it was from that sow, little brother!'

Luke was incensed, had a dollop of muck on the piece of timber he was using as a scraper and, without thinking, flipped it at Tate. It splatted against the rancher's shirt front and Luke only then realized what he had done. He dropped the board and leapt across the pen to the opposite side, flinging a leg over the top rail, but it was splintery and his trousers caught, holding him — just long enough for the raging Tate to reach him.

A big hand crashed across Luke's ear, bringing a howl of pain from him. It also knocked him off the fence and he sprawled on the ground. Tate lifted a boot to kick him but something made him pause and he set the foot down again, grabbed Luke's hair and pulled him brutally to his feet. He slapped the boy twice across the face, the shape of his fingers rising in red welts on Luke's freckled cheeks.

'Stop that! Stop that at once, Tate!'

They both looked up at the sound of

Annie's outraged voice. She had been watering her flower-garden just around the corner of the house when she heard the ruckus in the pig pen. Now she came running up.

'You're not supposed to leave the house, you know that!'

She stopped, panting, tight-lipped as she looked at her big brother. 'Leave Luke alone! You — you're nothing but a damn big bully, Tate Wilde! A mean, lousy bully, taking advantage . . . '

She reeled as he slapped her across the face. Luke swung at Tate but the big man dodged, knocked Luke down with a jarring blow. Tate put his hands on his hips, his raging gaze going from one to the other.

'So! We have a couple more rebels in the Wilde family, do we? Well, we'll soon put that to rights! You'll not only be locked in your rooms tonight, you'll go without supper — and breakfast, too, if I decide it!' He shook his head. 'It's about time you two realized I'm in charge here; you're both minors and I'll run your lives for you the way I see it until you reach twenty-one.' He smiled crookedly at Annie. 'And if you think you'll be able to go and marry Dan Dalton — well, think again, Annie dear! You'll never have him for a husband! And you, little brother? Oh, I've something special waiting for you, too!'

He grabbed each of them by an arm, sinking in his fingers, making them writhe as he started to drag them up towards the house. Luke tried to kick him and Annie tried to scratch his face. He laughed and shook them both brutally so that by the time they reached the house, tears were running down both their faces.

He flung Luke towards the wash bench. 'Get yourself cleaned up. Give him a hand, Annie. Consuela will be watching from the kitchen. She'll call me when you've finished.'

As Annie worked at washing some of the stains and muck off Luke's trousers, she said, trying to keep the sob out of her voice,

'We've got to get out of here, Luke! We've got to find Logan!' Then she started to weep. 'But what can we do, locked in our rooms? Tate's going to have the inside locks taken off and new ones put on the outside.'

Luke's face was dripping with water, still smeared a little with dirt. Annie impulsively gave him a hug, getting her own blouse wet and dirty.

Then suddenly he smiled. 'Don't worry about it, sis. Don't worry about anything!'

* * *

The scuffed riding-boot drove into Lennie Lawler's ribs and brought him out of his booze-induced doze with a shout of pain.

It was dark in the alley but he caught the silhouette of the big man standing over him. Lennie rubbed his aching ribs and swore, squinting. 'What the hell you doin', Rio?'

The big ramrod reached down and

pulled Lennie to his feet. He was a beefy man, too, and rapidly sobering now as Rio looked into his unshaven face. 'How drunk are you?'

'Not drunk enough. *Never* drunk enough, Rio!' Lennie grinned and chuckled — until Rio hooked him in the midriff.

'Well, are you sober enough to earn ten bucks?'

Lennie shook himself, wiped the back of a hairy wrist across his moist nostrils. 'By hell I am. What do I have to do?'

'Mebbe you can't do it alone, come to think of it,' Rio said. 'You might have to get Biff.'

'I ain't sharin' no ten bucks with Biff!'

'He can earn ten for himself. If he's sober enough to stick by you in a fight.'

Lennie reared back a little. 'I ain't lookin' for no fight tonight, Rio.'

'You want ten bucks, you'll fight.'

Lennie Lawler scraped a hand around his stubbled jowls. He licked his lips. Ten bucks would buy a lot of bar whiskey — better than drinking the dregs from the empties. 'Who we gotta beat up?'

Rio smiled slowly to himself. *Beat up? Those two rummies!* 'Just want you to kind of . . . soften him up a little. Keep him busy for a spell.'

Lennie grinned with his broken teeth. 'For you — an' the ten bucks — I'll do it, Rio!'

* * *

Logan Wilde didn't care for the night patrol but he was being paid to do a job and, like always, he would do it the best he knew how.

He had made the long, boring check of that part of the business section already closed, testing locks on the doors, moving on a few drunks. He had smoked a cigarette with the livery man, had a free drink at the bar of the Mother Lode, refused the attentions of one of the painted ladies: 'All free, honey, for our guardians of the law!' and moved on along Main. He passed a few minutes swapping hunting stories with the gunsmith and now was heading down Longhorn Street to the Aces High.

Dalton had warned him to be careful; several men who had had wins at the gambling-tables had been rolled in the alleys in the vicinity of the saloon. 'They ain't past clubbing a lawman investigating, either. Almost got my skull cracked once.'

The saloon was garish in its décor and the bar was separate to the gambling-rooms, which seemed like a good idea to Logan. If you wanted girls you had to climb the curving, ornate stairway to a red-and-gold draped reception area.

It had the smell of money and, standing against the wall just inside the gambling-room, Logan saw plenty changing hands. The drinks were kept flowing, oiling a few wallets as well as the gamblers' insides, encouraging recklessness with their bets. Of course, the house was usually on the winning side.

Logan strolled around, not disturbing anyone, though he got a few curious looks. Then suddenly the back door opened and a red-haired man in grubby clothes staggered in, shouting: 'Someone's gettin' the tar whaled outta them out here! Ah! Deputy. Just the man. Quick, before they kill him! He must've won a pot and they jumped him . . . '

No one else moved away from the gaming-tables but plenty looked at Logan who was already starting forward. The red-haired man had gone from the doorway and Logan went out cautiously, hand on gun butt.

He could hear the grunts and scuffling of a fight behind the stacked crates, glimpsed shadows of two men struggling.

'Quick! Before they kill him!' the red-haired man had shouted. They . . . But there were only two shadows scuffling around, if two were attacking, there should be three.

Then crates from the top of the stack fell all about him as the figures crashed into them. Logan jumped back but one crate hit his shoulder, taking him down to one knee.

Suddenly, the two shadows were charging him and in a shaft of light from the open saloon door he glimpsed red hair. The man picked up another crate and threw it at him. Logan fell trying to dodge. Then they were upon him, kicking and slugging, one man wielding an empty bottle by the neck. Logan lashed out and the bottle shattered as it flew from the man's hand. He yelled in pain and his companion drove a kick at Logan's head.

He rolled away, got to all fours, charged forward from a crouching position, arms spread wide, taking down both men. The smell of booze on their breaths was mighty strong but it didn't seem to interfere in any way with what they had set out to do. They stumbled and rolled and yelled and more crates tumbled down on top of all three. Logan threw himself aside, bounced up and smashed Lennie Lawler in the middle of the face.

Lennie howled as his nose crunched and blood spurted. He staggered into Biff's path and the red-head shoved him aside roughly, swung at Logan, missed by a foot. Logan buried his fist to the wrist in his midriff. Biff dropped to his knees, retching, and Lennie, making a belated and futile comeback, snatched up another empty bottle, flung it at Logan who dodged easily. The deputy started forward but Lennie had had enough and began to run. Biff stumbled to his feet and, half-doubled over, lurched away, too.

Logan didn't aim to expend any more energy on a couple of drunks putting him to the test, which was how he saw the set-up. He picked up his hat and set it on his head.

A gun blasted out of the darkness at the far end of the saloon's lot and splinters flew from a crate at head-height. Down full length on the ground, Logan snapped a shot at where he had seen the muzzle flash, spun swiftly aside as three bullets slammed into the soft earth beside him.

He came up on one knee, triggered two fast shots at the gunman's position, lunged to the side, and began to run down behind a line of stacked kegs and more crates. Whoever it was heard him coming and took off after another wild shot. Logan halted just before the end of the line of kegs and a bullet whined off; the killer had been hoping to nail him as he emerged from the cover of the barrels.

The man was running now, feet pounding through weeds which told Logan he was heading for the back of the business section. Might even have a mount waiting . . .

He was right. He heard the small whinny of the horse as the man came out of the darkness and leapt into the saddle. He wheeled and spurred away.

Logan raised his gun but held his fire. It was too damn dark! Solid blackness back here, away from the glow of the streetlights.

So he turned and ran back fast, catching the redhead as the man tried to find his way through the piles of fallen crates and kegs. He spun the man and hit him in the face. Biff went down hard and Logan hauled him up by his shirt front, shook him violently, ramming his gunsmoke-reeking Colt muzzle into the man's blood-streaked face.

'Who paid you to jump me?' Biff shook his head and Logan turned the gun barrel so the blade foresight was pushing painfully into Biff's flesh. 'One good jerk and your face'll split open like a ripe peach!'

'Hold it! For Chris'sakes, man. I dunno. *No*! Gospel! Someone paid Lennie an' me to jump you! I dunno who it was, but Lennie, goddamn him, has lit out with my ten bucks!'

'You can do better than that, Red.

Next time you look in the mirror, you'll wish you had!'

'Wait! Hell. I — I think it was Rio. From Block W.'

Logan nodded. Yeah! It would be like Rio, get a couple of drunks to jump him, then while they were keeping him busy, he'd put a bullet into Logan. Maybe the drunks as well.

He shoved the red-head aside and turned down the alley beside the saloon, seeing the crowd of gawkers pouring out of the rear door.

Minutes later, he rode out of town.

He still recalled the short cuts to Block W from seven years ago, but Rio didn't seem to be using them. Likely he was taking the regular trail, hoping Logan would pursue him that way, might even set up an ambush.

Well, Rio could spend the night waiting for Logan to appear, while the deputy followed the old shortcuts all the way to Block W.

He had unfinished business there and didn't aim to put it off any longer.

12

Night of the Hunters

Reining down the big dun he had borrowed from the livery, Logan wondered if it had been such a good idea to come out here to the ranch.

He figured with Rio in town, trying to backshoot him, that the nighthawks and line guards would slacken off and he would be able to slip in and maybe find a way to reach Annie and Luke, get them out of Tate's clutches.

Then he could concentrate of squaring things with his brother and Ash McGowan.

He remembered one time hearing McGowan boast in a bar that some day he would run Cedar County, appointing his own judges and law officials, living the high life, a latter-day emperor. He had just closed a big deal and had been drinking to celebrate, so no one took him seriously, but the years passed and Ash quietly acquired more and more of the county, gaining power. Was it possible he was obsessive or manic enough to really try to bring his fantasy to life?

Logan knew McGowan would want his bite — a big bite — at the cake that was Block W, and he would have covered himself from all angles so everything would appear above-board. He was so arrogant he believed that he alone could accomplish what he wanted; hired help was never good enough. He might use Rio or some other fast gun if necessary, but it would be strictly on a temporary basis. He had been here a long time and must have many favours he could call in, or plenty of folk he could blackmail into helping him.

People didn't realize he had this county by the neck. No other attorney had ever made more than a bread-and-butter living in Cedar Butte, and only stayed operational for as long as

McGowan dictated. Some even had their offices burnt down. So Ash *knew* about people and their affairs — people who had little choice but to have dealings with him. He might not always be successful first time, but eventually he got what he wanted. If someone had to fall along the way, all the angles would be covered and no one could point at McGowan and say, let alone *prove*, that he had broken the law. McGowan would use any means to keep his well-nourished hide safe.

But the main thing now for Logan was to do what he could for *his* kinfolk.

Patting the sweating neck of the dun, listening to it breathing deeply and steadily from the fast ride out here, Logan watched the outline of the hogback rising against the stars. He hadn't been mistaken: there were horsemen riding along the crest, other men on foot, working the slopes, the latter using blazing pine-cone torches as they examined the ground. *Hunting something — or someone!* Maybe a wolf or coyote worrying the herd?

He dropped a hand to his gun butt as a twig cracked over to his right. A man afoot came groping out of the bushes, stopped dead when he saw Logan's silhouette.

'What the hell you doin', still on your hoss?' the man demanded in a gravelly voice. 'Tate said to work this part on foot and — *Judas*!'

The cowboy must have suddenly realized he wasn't talking to one of the Block W riders. He jumped back, fumbling for his sixgun. Logan jammed home the spurs and the big dun gave a protesting whinny as it leapt forward, and sent the cowboy reeling. Logan was out of the saddle in a blur of speed, kicked the man in the side, crashed his head against a tree. The cowboy groaned but still brought up his pistol. Logan's Colt whispered out of leather and cracked across his head. The cowboy dropped, moaning, hat rolling off.

Logan threw him down on his back.

He leaned forward, waving the gun an inch from the ranny's contorted, blood-streaked face. 'What's going on?'

'Hell almighty! It's — you're Logan, ain't you?'

'You better believe it, mister.' He didn't know the cowboy so he likely hadn't been working here seven years ago. 'What're you searching for?'

'You. If you got any sense, you'll light a shuck! The whole crew's out. They'll shoot you on sight.'

Logan cocked the hammer slowly, close to the man's ear. But he was game enough, lying there bleeding, head buzzing like a hornet's nest, throbbing like a medicine-show drum.

'You won't shoot! The rest'll be down on your neck, if you do. So what you gonna do?'

'I'll fix it so you never walk again without a stick.'

As he spoke Logan placed the muzzle of the Colt against the man's right knee-cap, heard his gasp, felt him try to move his leg away. 'I'll take my chances with your pards.'

'Christ! It ain't worth it. We're lookin' for the kids.'

Logan felt a tightening in his belly. 'Annie and Luke?'

'Yeah. Tate locked 'em in their rooms but they got free. Ike Wilson was takin' a leak, saw 'em tryin' to get hosses from the corral and they run off.'

'They're afoot?'

'Yeah. Last Wilson seen of 'em, they was headed into the ranges. He an' a couple others been makin' hooch; he was half-drunk, took his time wakin' Tate, an' got reamed out for the delay.'

Logan had heard enough. He lowered his gun hammer and slammed the barrel across the luckless cowboy's head again. The man slumped, and Logan thumbed back his hat, turning to the waiting dun. Hell! Annie and Luke afoot, at night in the hills, with up to twenty men searching for them. They wouldn't know what to do, where to hide.

Wait! They must both know the country pretty well. Annie was a good rider and Luke, too. He guessed Annie and Dalton must have met somewhere out here, somewhere private with a good view of the approaches so they could be warned in plenty of time if Tate sent someone searching.

Luke used to be adventurous, like any ten-year-old, prowling the river banks with a fishing-pole and blanket, staying out overnight and getting the tar whaled out of him by Pa if he was caught sneaking back. So, come to think of it, they both must know some pretty good hiding-places.

Trouble was, Logan didn't know where they were; seven years dodging bullets and *rurales* south of the Rio had seen to that. So, where to start?

One thing he did know: he had better get the hell out of here before any more of the Block W crew saw him.

* * *

At that moment, the fugitives were a long way from the hogback rise where

Logan had encountered the unknown cowboy.

The search seemed to be confined to the hills closest to the pastures and the ranch itself, Tate working on the theory that Annie and Luke couldn't travel far on foot, especially in the dark.

But Tate didn't know his little brother very well.

Nor did Annie, come to that. She had been lying awake on her bed in the locked room, crumpling a damp handkerchief in hands that wouldn't keep still. She had tried not to give way but she couldn't help crying a little.

She wanted Dan Dalton so badly! Wanted to feel his strong arms around her, holding her — *safe*. And she wanted to see Logan; he had always been a tower of strength, even when he was thought to be reckless and a local hell-raiser. Tate was just awful. He had always been short-tempered, easily hurt, resentful, convinced he worked harder than anyone else on the Block W. It was true that Pa did drive him roughly, especially after Logan went to Mexico. But he was hard on them all from that time. He would never admit it, but Logan's absence was like a knife in the Old Man's heart. Marsh Wilde had favoured Logan because he had so closely resembled a young brother, also named Logan, who had died tragically in his twenties. Tate had resented that more than she and Luke; perhaps with good reason, because, as the eldest, more was expected of him. And Pa, never really getting over the death of their mother, would never let up on driving Tate.

'I almost killed myself,' he used to roar at Tate when he found something to criticize — and that was *all* the time, 'buildin' up this place for my wife and kids. Ma's gone, may the Lord bless her, and — and so has Logan, gone in a different sense, but gone nonetheless. That leaves you, the one with muscles and the so-called 'brains'. So you keep this ranch the way I made it — or make it better! You got no other choice, boy!'

Annie thought that her father must be preparing Tate to take over the spread when he died, but Tate had actually caused him more worry than Logan, who was considered to be the wildest one of the Wilde family.

Tate always claimed he was underpaid; or, at least, never given enough money so he could have a good time in town. Maybe that had started him gambling: a desperate attempt to fund his own pleasure, the 'easy' way. Which, of course, turned out to be anything but, once Tate began signing IOUs. She knew it had something to do with that wealthy attorney, McGowan, but, still seen as a child, she was never given details, knew only that Tate had brought more worry and trouble for the family. If not downright shame.

Marshall Wilde was about ready to make some sort of move to straighten things out when he had run that rusty nail into his hand, and then it was too late.

She had reached this point in her musings on her bed in the darkened room when she thought she heard some small noise at the door. Annie tensed, listening. The sound continued but she couldn't place it or identify it. *Mouse . . . ?*

Bosom heaving, she sat up on the edge of the bed as the door eased open. Vast relief flooded her as Luke slipped in, screwdriver in one hand, the new outside lock in the other. He grinned, speaking in a whisper.

'Big brother made a mistake, putting the locks on the outside so we couldn't work on 'em and try to open 'em from inside our rooms. He screwed 'em to the door.' He waved the screwdriver. 'Took about two minutes to take it off.'

'But how did you get out of your room? All our windows are nailed shut!'

'Aw, I've had a getaway hole for years, since I used to sneak out to go night fishing with Ray Scully. I found that some loose boards in the back of the clothes' closet led to a space between the walls; you know, where Pa added that split-log outer wall so as to keep the house warmer in winter. I climbed down once — it's only a few feet — and found a way under the logs. Come on, sis, let's move.'

It was as easy as he made it sound. Within fifteen minutes Luke had screwed the lock back into place on the outside of Annie's door, then led the way through the silent house to a cobwebbed, disused storage space in back of the kitchen. In a couple of minutes they were outside the big house. Annie sneezed, brushed dirt from her clothes. They hurried towards the corrals.

Luke surprised her again after Wilson spotted them and they had to make a run for it: he led the way to an old sheet-iron-and-fruitbox canoe hidden above the river in the brush. He told her that he and Ray Scully had used it in their nocturnal fishing adventures, long ago.

They paddled a long way from the home pastures of Block W before some of the rust patches gave way and caused the canoe to leak. They ran it aground before it could sink, dragged it up, covered it with bushes, then hurried into the trees.

'Do you know where we are?' Annie panted and Luke stopped, breathing hard, too. She saw his arm swing across the stars as he pointed.

'The trail to town lies over there somewhere. But we'd never get that far on foot. They'll overtake us once they realize we aren't in the hills. We'd have to cross V-Bar-G first, too. I'm not sure which way to go now, sis.'

She patted his arm, smiling. 'You've done very well indeed, Luke. Logan and Pa would be proud of you. I know I am.' She saw the flash of his teeth as he smiled at her compliment. 'I think we should call on Val Guthrie.'

He stiffened. 'Why? She keeps herself to herself, minds her own business. She won't help us.'

'I think she might. I've had a little to do with her and she's not as hard as she makes out.'

He seemed hesitant, but then said, 'Well, I guess we've got nothing to lose. She'll either offer us sanctuary or send us on our way. We won't be any worse off than we are now.'

She took his hand and they started moving away from the river, towards wilder country.

* * *

The cowboy whom Logan had slugged regained consciousness slowly, his head all a-thunder, senses oscillating like a porch swing in a storm. His name was Hedder, and he knew cattle and this country, though he showed little aptitude for anything else than cowboying.

But, perhaps having a hard head — as some of the other cowpokes maintained — was to his advantage right now. He recovered from Logan's gunwhipping faster than most of his pards would have done, then stumbled his way towards the hogback rise. The searchers there had moved over the crest to the far side by now. Panting and gasping, he half-crawled up the slope and at the top, rose up shouting:

'Logan's here! He gunwhipped me!'

Men came running and riding in from all directions, most shouting the same thing: 'Where the hell is he?'

'Dunno — but he's after them kids, too.'

A gruff voice said. 'He's got a thousand-buck bounty ridin' him! Me, I'll go lookin' for Logan. Hell with the kids!'

That was the general feeling, and in seconds the slopes and brush and timber were alive with riders; those afoot hurried to where they had ground-hitched their mounts. Gun metal glinted in the starlight. There was no more shouting: it was every man for himself.

Not one of them even considered splitting the bounty with anyone else.

* * *

Logan had heard the rough voices calling when Hedder had come round and raised the alarm. Then there was no further exchange of words, but they weren't making much effort to keep their mounts quiet.

So now his plans for the night had blown up in his face. He hoped Annie and Luke were well away from here by now. It would be hell's own luck for them to be discovered accidentally by the Block W searchers out for his scalp.

He knew these hills well enough in the daylight but wasn't as confident at night. Some of the landmarks had changed over the years; mostly timber had grown up and taken on a different profile from what he recalled; rocks had fallen during weathering, changing silhouettes.

In daylight he could work things out. Now, well, he could use general directions, but would be better off sticking to Block W pastures, finding his way back into the foothills from there. These cowpokes worked the hills every day of their lives so they had the advantage. *And* a $1,000 motive driving them.

Thinking this out, he was working the dun down into a brush-walled gulch. The animal lurched as it stepped down from one level to the one below. He heard the whip of the bullet passing over his head at the same time as the crack of the hidden rifle. That lurch had saved his neck, but the shot would bring in the hunters like the clanging of the ranch triangle announcing it was pay-day.

For most of them, they were hoping it would be just that.

But he had wheeled the dun, almost upsetting it as it was still finding firm footing, when the rifle crashed again. Out of his left eye he caught the muzzle flash; someone had known of this gulch and beat him to it, set up an ambush amongst the tumbled boulders and brush at the far end.

Luckily, the slope behind him was dark with brush so he was not silhouetted. The bullets missed; after the third shot he realized the rifleman was shooting wild, had no idea where Logan had gone. He was leaning forward, stroking the dun's quivering neck and gently talking into its ear, keeping it calm while he figured out what to do.

There were distant, discordant shouts drifting through the night. Logan's Colt was in his hand, cocked and ready as he looked about him. It was too damn dark, but he searched his memory, placing this gulch in a remembered aspect in relation to the ranch house.

He figured he had it, and there wasn't any easy way out except a blind charge and raking spurs, not to mention a blazing gun.

If he jumped the dun out of this hollow right now, he might just make it before the others thundering in could trap him. The spurs were raking even before the thought had fully formed. The dun protested with a whinnying toss of its head and Logan felt the hard skull just brush his jaw. A little harder and he would have been unseated.

But the dun was a working cattle horse and instinctively responded with a forward lunge that caught Logan unawares and sent him lurching upright. Guns from three different directions opened up and he lashed with the rein ends, held his fire, concentrating on getting out of the gulch. Using the gun flashes as marks, he figured that with a little luck he might just make it before they closed in and trapped him where they could pick him off at their leisure.

Then the dun burst through the last screen of brush and Logan had a blurred sense of movement coming across at him from the right; he ducked low as a gun hammered. Sliding slightly to the far side he thumbed off three shots.

There was a startled cry, a thrashing and whinnying of a horse, its rider cursing, and the unmistakable sounds of a mount going down. Just in time he lifted the dun over the thrashing, sliding heap and spun in the saddle as another rider came slanting in from upslope.

The newcomer threw up a rifle and, still crouched low in leather, Logan triggered. He saw the man's arms jump violently upward across the stars and then the body toppled sideways. Someone yelled behind him and two guns crashed. He used knees and reins and curses to weave the dun through the brush. A man on foot leapt for his reins and Logan wrenched the dun slightly; the impact hurled the cowboy at least six feet.

More guns hammered on the slopes now, but he knew they couldn't see him down here in the darkness. Even so, several bullets came mighty close. Leaving the gulch behind now, he swung left, then hard right, just as someone fired a rifle only yards upslope. The Colt bucked in his hand and he saw ragged movement up there, heard a startled shout.

Then he was past the brush into the edge of the timber. But he only held this dangerous path, ducking low-swinging branches, for a few yards, then veered out into the open and saw something glinting. The river!

Better than he could have hoped for. He knew where he was now, could even see the open country that led away to Val Guthrie's place.

He knew where he could cross without being seen by the fools who were yelling at each other from various parts of Block W. V-Bar-G would offer him some kind of sanctuary, even if only for long enough to pick up a fresh mount.

He wouldn't make it too hard for his pursuers; if he could draw them after him, Annie and Luke would stand a better chance of escape.

The river crossing went off successfully. He dodged the hunters who seemed incapable of keeping quiet now and urged the dripping dun up the bank, riding on to to Guthrie land.

Then two riders came out from behind the trees, rifles raised.

'Where the hell you think you're goin', Wilde man?'

13

Judgement Day

It wasn't until they took him back to the Guthrie bunkhouse and got a light that one of the riflemen, Lefty, recognized Logan.

'Hell, we thought you were just one of the Block W rannies on the trail of them kids.'

'They've been hunting me. S'pose you've heard Tate has a bounty on me?'

Lefty's young face puckered in a smile. 'You like to live dangerously, huh? I mean, we could collect that bounty, now you told us about it.'

Logan gave him back a little of the smile. 'You could try, I guess.'

Lefty pursed his lips, swivelled his eyes to the other man, medium tall but solidly built. 'Think we should, Eli?'

'Think *you* should, if you want. Me, I

recall what happened to Pike and Rowdy.'

Lefty sighed. 'OK, we'll leave him be.'

Logan gestured to the empty bunk-house. 'Where's the rest of the crew?'

'Out on the lines watchin' Block W don't trespass. A couple are in the house with Val, guardin' them kids.'

'Glad to hear they made it. I'd like to see 'em.'

Lefty held a gun on Logan, very casually, while Eli checked with Val. When Logan walked into the lamplit parlour, Annie, her wrinkled clothes soiled with dirt and twigs, ran across the room and threw her arms about his neck.

'Oh! Thank *goodness* you're here, Logan!'

He smiled, and Luke came up, solemnly held out a hand which Logan gripped. 'You two've done right well.' He flicked his gaze to Val Guthrie who stood beside a stuffed sofa, the leather covering cracked here and there, one overpatch sewn on reasonably professionally. There was also a Colt and a Winchester carbine resting on it. '*Muchas gracias*, Val, for taking them in.'

'They are two of the Wildes whom I trust. There is a third, though.' She allowed herself a slow smile. 'You probably know it's not Tate.'

'Be surprised if it was. But by taking 'em in, you've declared your hand. It'll be open war with Block W now.'

'I was rather depending on you to see that didn't happen, Logan.'

She was shrewd all right: she had seen that once he knew Annie and Luke were safe, then he was free to go after Tate and Ash McGowan, or anyone else he saw as an enemy.

'You'll keep them here?'

She nodded.

'Tate's got men hunting all over the range. Only a matter of time before they come here to check.'

'We're prepared.'

'They could be more interested in me

than Annie and Luke just now. You know about the bounty?'

Val nodded slowly. 'Your own brother, putting a dead-or-alive price on your head! It's shameful!'

Logan shrugged. 'Tate's got a lot to lose — or gain, depending which side you happen to be standing on.'

'For heaven's sake! Don't make little of it! It's your *life* at stake here!'

He scratched his stubbled jaw. 'Well, I'm as shook up as you are, but that don't change anything.'

Her eyes narrowed. 'Isn't changing things why you're here?'

Logan grinned. 'By Godfrey, you don't let up, do you? I didn't come back to change anything. I thought Pa was still alive and I wanted to see him. I wanted to set a few things straight.'

She studied him closely. 'Then . . . ?'

'Well, I wasn't about to go back to Mexico. Kind of wore out my welcome there. I guess I would've just moved on; it's a big country.'

'Now?'

'Same thing, except I have to make sure Annie and Luke's futures are set before I go anywhere.'

For the first time since he had been brought in, Val's face softened and there was genuine warmth in her eyes for him. 'I have only a few men, but if you need any help . . . ?'

'No. This is my chore.'

'Don't I have a say in this?' Annie spoke up and Luke hurriedly added, '*And* me!'

'No, kids. Your hearts are in the right places, but it's a gun that's needed here, not a heart. Suits me better.'

Annie smiled at him. 'Oh, you darn liar, Logan Wilde!' She turned to Val. 'Can you believe that?'

Val Guthrie's eyes crinkled. 'I . . . think perhaps Logan meant a gun's needed as *well* as a heart.'

'What I need is a fresh mount — and maybe some ammunition,' Logan told them roughly. 'Can't stand here gabbing all night.'

Lefty pulled the window drape aside

a few inches. 'Be light in a couple hours.'

'Then I'd best get moving.'

* * *

Tate Wilde stared blearily at the half-empty bottle of bourbon resting on his desk. He was red-eyed, and had a foul taste in his mouth.

He had been sitting here for hours, drinking, and worrying. Now he noticed a patch of grey outlining the eastern window. He jumped when the door crashed open and big Rio stomped in, clothes torn here and there from rough passage through brush and timber, a look of murder on his heavy features.

'Christ! I din' believe Jingo when he told me you'd been suckin' redeye all damn night!' The ramrod stepped across, picked up the bottle and swigged straight from it, smacking his lips. 'I needed that. So, the kids got away and Logan came back, shot-up the crew, and now is God-knows-where, no doubt raisin' hell — for *us*!'

Tate frowned and held his head. 'Shut up yelling! If you'd finished him in town we wouldn't be in this fix.'

'Aaah. Was Lennie Lawler and that damn Biff. They was too drunk to start with. Then thought I could draw Logan into an ambush on the trail but he never showed — too busy leadin' the crew away from them damn kids, I s'pose.'

Tate waved lazily. 'Kids can't prove nothing. Ash'll see to that.'

Rio swore. 'Judas, Tate! It's likely the kids are at the Guthrie place. Logan knows they'll be safe there and he's gonna come after us — or McGowan.'

'Ash'll take care of Logan.'

Rio almost spat. 'That hunk of flab!'

'He's a lot tougher'n he looks.' Tate cleared his throat, fighting to think clearly. 'That old maid works for him — Miss Harper — she knows too much. Ash says it's time she had an . . . accident. A fatal one.'

Rio frowned but said nothing.

'But there'll be clues that point to her

having been murdered, and the killer tried to make it look like an accident.'

'Well, I guess that's the kind of thing Ash can handle, but — '

'*But*!' Tate said with a crooked grin. 'The clues will point to Logan!' He spread his hands, let them fall back in his lap. 'There'll be witnesses and everything. Logan will hang, or get years in jail. We'll have no more problems.'

Rio looked doubtful. 'Too easy. What clues, anyway?'

'Plenty. Logan left a lot of stuff here: clasp-knife with his name engraved on it, neckerchief Ma made him and embroidered his initials in a corner — got torn when he took a fall one round-up, but he kept it. Lots of other stuff that can be traced back to him.'

Rio seemed less sceptical now. 'When's it happen?'

Tate made a couple of attempts before he heaved to his feet, swaying. 'I'm s'posed to take the stuff in this morning. You ride with me.'

Rio grinned crookedly. 'Just in case we run into Logan, eh? Suits me, Tate. Suits me fine.'

* * *

In the dim light of early morning, Miss Harper crouched in front of McGowan's large desk, a yellowed envelope in her trembling hands. Under the lower drawer, a false wooden bottom sloped to the floor. She had remembered seeing McGowan hurriedly closing this a couple of years ago, and now had managed at last to locate and open it.

She partly drew out the papers in the envelope, smiled faintly. 'I knew it! Marshall Wilde's original will.' She drew it out all the way and, still crouching, began to read.

She was absorbed in what she was reading and didn't hear the outside door at the top of the stairs open. But a small gust of cool early-morning air blew in and made her snap her head up.

'Well, Miss Harper, you seem to be

making a habit of opening my office much earlier than usual.'

She began to shake and fumbled her efforts at trying to return the will to the envelope. Ash McGowan almost filled the doorway. He came forward, one big hand reaching out.

'I'll take that.'

She stood hurriedly, feeling light-headed, knowing her blood pressure was acting up again. She steadied herself on the edge of the desk, moving to keep it between her and the advancing attorney.

McGowan looked very frightening, his eyes narrowed, thick lips thinned out, an implacability in his stride as she backed away. She clung to the envelope, holding it in front of her bosom as if it was some kind of shield.

'You nosy old bitch! I should've got rid of you years ago, but you knew too damn much about my business!' He advanced and smiled coldly. 'As usual, I prefer to take care of problems myself. Now . . . '

‘I — I always respected your confidences, Mr McGowan!’ she said in a shaky voice, backing away. ‘You know I can be trusted.’

‘You have been trustworthy,’ he admitted. ‘But this is my biggest and potentially most profitable project. Block W is the key to this entire county. I can’t afford to risk anything that may prevent me having it.’

The big hand was still reaching out in front of him and he snapped thick fingers, giving her a bleak smile. ‘Give me the envelope! Perhaps we can talk about this in a civilized manner.’

She shook her head, clutched the envelope more tightly, edging around the walls towards her own desk. ‘This isn’t right, Mr McGowan! You are destroying a family here, a family who have supported you over the years. Why, I recall Marsh Wilde even lending you money that time you — ’

‘I have no interest in the past!’ he snapped, mouth opening and closing like a steel trap. ‘You are a danger to me now and I will — not — tolerate it! *Give me that envelope!'*

She made a small whining sound, feinted a move that would take her behind her desk. He fell for it and lunged, and she pushed her lighter desk hard, pinning him against the wall. Miss Harper, sobbing in fear, ran for the door at the top of the stairs. McGowan, swearing as he struggled to free himself, snatched a heavy glass pen-rest from the desk and threw it. It struck her between the shoulders and she cried out as she stumbled, went down on all fours, half in and half out of the office.

With a roar and a burst of desperate strength, McGowan heaved the desk aside and, free at last, raging, charged after the old woman as she started to rise shakily.

Right in front of him.

He reached for her with both hands, aiming to pick her up and throw her over the landing rail. But she was too close and he tripped, fell across her instead. Both cried out, Miss Harper gasping under his crushing weight.

But it was only a brief discomfort. McGowan's momentum carried him across the landing. He crashed into the slim railings and his great weight splintered the wood. Flailing, screaming, he plunged to the ground below.

There was a heavy thud, a *cracking* sound and then silence. Shuddering, sobbing, Miss Harper dragged herself forward, still clinging to the envelope with one hand, and looked over the edge apprehensively.

Ash McGowan was sprawled face down, one leg at an odd angle, both feet twisted abnormally, blood around his head. She couldn't tell if he was alive or dead.

Exhausted, feeling her old heart thudding violently against her ribs, she sat back against the wall, legs lying straight out in front of her on the landing, the envelope unnoticed in her lap as she closed her eyes.

* * *

When she opened them again, she was sitting in Ash McGowan's padded desk chair, coughing as smooth brandy caught the back of her throat. She pushed the small glass away from her mouth, automatically reached for the scented lace handkerchief in the cuff of her long-sleeved blouse and dabbed her lips.

An image swam into focus and she sucked in a sharp breath, dizziness making her grab at the arms of the chair.

'Logan!' Her voice was a soft whisper. What colour there was drained from her face and she sat up straighter. 'Oh, my! I — remember now. Is — is Mr McGowan . . . ?'

'He's alive. I'd say he's got some busted ribs and two smashed ankles, maybe a head injury. Forget about him. You did well, Miss Harper.'

She shook her head vehemently. 'No, no! I — I didn't push or throw him off the landing! He — he tripped over me and . . . ' Her eyes went to the splintered railings.

'By the look of the office there was a struggle. You got nothing to worry about, Miss Harper. No one'll blame you. Would you like another brandy? Or I can fetch Doc Hershey . . . ?'

'Mr McGowan might — benefit from the doctor?'

'He's unconscious. Leave him be for a spell.' Logan held up the torn envelope. 'I read a little. It's Pa's original, I guess.'

She nodded. 'And — and the sad part about it is that Marsh left the ranch to you and Tate in equal shares, with Annie and Luke each to have a specified percentage of the ranch upon reaching their majority. It was a very fair distribution of assets, Logan. I don't understand why Tate wouldn't have been satisfied with it.'

'Well, I wasn't here. I guess Tate figured he deserved *all* of Block W. He needed it to trade off his gambling debts with McGowan. He might've even seen that McGowan would take it all eventually, but as long as he had outstanding IOUs there wasn't much he could do about it.'

She studied him carefully. 'I think you are being too generous.'

'How so?'

'Tate. He resented you and the others. He did not intend that any of you should have any share in Block W. Why, he even went so far as to put a bounty on you!'

Logan was grim-faced and silent. She was right, or partly so. Tate likely would never have done any actual harm to Luke or Annie, but neither would have seen their inheritance, either. As for Logan, well, more than likely, Tate had never thought Logan would be any real problem, that he would remain in Mexico — an outcast.

Now, the way things had gone, Tate had no option but to kill Logan, or die trying.

And Logan didn't want it that way. But he would fight Tate every inch of the way to make sure that Annie and

Luke were treated fairly and got their full rights.

He took Miss Harper to Doc Hershey. The medic ordered her home to bed, arranged for a nurse to call in and take care of her for a few days.

McGowan was brought to the infirmary, still unconscious. Hershey was mixing plaster to make casts for his ankles and one arm. The man's head and ribs were already heavily bandaged; he might or might not pull through. Logan went to Dalton, who could get around reasonably well on crutches now.

They read the will and Dalton said, 'You'll have to prove the new one is a fake before this becomes legal.'

Logan nodded. 'Miss Harper'll be able to do that, all right. What about Tate, Dan?'

Dalton gave him a strange look. 'I know he's your brother, Logan — and Annie's, too.'

'And your future brother-in-law.'

'Reckon I could be happy without

him as that, but he was in on the fraud, even though he might've been put under pressure by McGowan with those IOUs. And he's tried to have you killed. Which might not be all that easy to prove.'

'Why don't you leave him to me?'

Dalton's gaze was steady. 'As a deputy? Or brother?'

'Just as Logan Wilde.'

Dan pursed his lips. 'I think mebbe Tate has gone a mite too far for blood to matter much to him, unless it's yours, and spilled aplenty.'

'I need to square up to Tate, Dan.'

'You do, there'll be trouble. But you know that, *expect* it.' He paused. 'I don't believe you'll trade lead with Tate, Logan.'

'Well, I wouldn't just stand still while he shot at me.'

''Course not. What I'm sayin' is, Tate's a sore loser. And he knows he could never outdraw or outshoot you.'

'Rio?'

Dan Dalton shrugged. 'He's the

Block W troubleshooter. You be careful. I wouldn't mind *you* for a brother-in-law.'

Logan smiled, clapped Dalton on the shoulder. 'Knew you had good taste.'

* * *

They met on the bridge at the end of Main Street.

Shade trees had been planted at either end of the humpbacked bridge and there were stretches of grass and coarse sand on each bank of the river for families to picnic and attend celebrations, like Independence Day and the Thanksgiving luncheon the Cedar Butte Progress Committee put on each year.

Logan had seen them riding out of the sun, still early and without much heat in it. He pulled off to the side and sat the high-stepping roan Val Guthrie had given him in the deep shadow of the overhanging willow branches.

Tate looked kind of hungover and

miserable. Logan had seen him like that countless times and knew his mood would be mean and spiteful until he had recovered. Rio rode alongside, slack in the saddle, eyes darting, hand never far from his gun butt.

It was Rio who spotted the roan. He reined down, one hand slapping the butt of his Colt. 'Logan!' he gritted.

Tate, startled, hauled rein violently, almost pulling his horse up on to its hindlegs. He grabbed at his rifle in the scabbard as the horse came down with a jolt.

Logan walked the roan out, right hand on his thigh. 'Easy, gents. Palaver, not pistols, if you don't mind.'

Rio exchanged a hard look with Tate. 'Call it, damnit! It's gotta end here! *Right now*!'

Tate hesitated, licked his lips, and Rio swore, spun his horse, palming up his Colt and snapping a shot across his body at Logan, who stretched out along the roan, using his spurs.

Rio's shot missed but he was still

shooting as he rode his mount towards Logan. He stood in the stirrups, leaning forward, so eager was he to shoot Logan out of the saddle. A bullet clipped Logan's left ear and he felt a spray of warm blood on his neck. He leaned to the side and fired two fast shots under the mount's arching neck. The animal shied and swayed but one slug hit home, rocking Rio in his saddle.

He clung tightly, hipped around and threw down with his last shots. Logan triggered simultaneously and Rio lurched, was slammed sideways out of leather. Another bullet punched him clear of the horse. His body struck the stone rail, skidded along, writhing, and dropped over into the river, landing amidst large rocks. The horse ran on and Tate took advantage of it, levered and triggered his rifle. Lead spat dust around the roan's feet, another ripped Logan's hat from his head and he was too late to dodge Rio's frightened horse.

It hit the roan and both mounts, and

Logan, went down in a thrashing tangle. Logan rolled away from the flailing hoofs and Tate spurred forward, shooting down with the rifle. The bullet ripped a red scar across Logan's cheek and his head jerked. He kept rolling, shooting wild, just to keep Tate's horse from stomping him. *He had to keep moving — or die.*

But Tate saw his chance, bared his teeth and reared his horse up on to its hindlegs. The forelegs beat the air as it shrilled and slammed down, the shoes striking sparks from the crushed-stone pathway. A piece of gravel hit Logan in the corner of his left eye and his vision blurred. He spun to the left and Tate drove home the spurs, urging the mount after him, intending to crush his brother under the hoofs.

Logan slammed into the stone wall and realized he had nowhere else to go. He brought up his Colt, but the hammer fell on an empty chamber and he knew everything was going to end, right here, right now.

Tate grinned in anticipation, then the grin changed to a fleeting mask of agony as his head jerked violently and blood and bone burst in a reddish mist from his right temple. Tate spilled sideways, crashing to the ground within a yard of where Logan lay, never to move again, his head shattered.

Frowning, shaken, Logan clawed to his feet and saw a man standing at the town end of the bridge, a smoking rifle in hand. The fore-end was resting across the padded top of a crutch, a second crutch under Dan Dalton's left arm giving him support while he had made his shot.

'Told you I didn't fancy him as a brother-in-law.'

Logan lifted a hand in acknowledgement, glanced down at Tate while he reloaded, and saw the citizens of Cedar Butte who had been awakened by the shooting, crowding down towards the bridge.

Logan caught the roan and swung wearily up into the saddle, blood rivulets snaking across his gaunt face. He looked down at Dalton.

'I'm riding out to Val Guthrie's. Annie and Luke are there. Can you ride yet?'

'I'm about to find out. Come on down to the livery with me. Might have to hire a rig.'

'Whatever suits you, though I have the notion you'll crawl if there's no other option.'

Dalton gave one of his rare smiles.

'Every inch of the way — through Wilde country.'

THE END

Other titles in the
Linford Western Library:

REDEMPTION IN INFERNO

H. H. Cody

Lew Faulds got himself talked into taking the job of deputy sheriff in the town of Blind Bend by his two-timing sweetheart. However, he had no idea the job would get him into so much trouble. A set of outlaws came to town and killed the sheriff. Then they put a hunk of lead into Lew's hand, figuring they'd crippled him. Scared, Lew ran, only to meet up with a stranger who helped him out. Now the pair went hunting the outlaws and caught up with them in the town of Inferno. Would they survive the showdown and would Lew regain his self respect?

OWLHOOT BANDITS

David Bingley

When ex-Cavalry officer Lieutenant Bob McCleave hurries home to the Diamond M in Rockwall County, New Mexico, it's because his father's freight business is under threat. Approaching home, Bob clashes with freight raiders at Indian Ridge. But when it appears that it's the local banks that are now at risk, he becomes a temporary deputy. After a renegade outfit raids the South-Western National in Broad Creek, will Bob's ruthlessness and shooting accuracy be enough to overthrow those responsible?

THE BOUNTY KILLERS

Owen G. Irons

Most bounty hunters operated legally to bring their quarries to justice 'dead or alive'. But for Big Jack Corrigan however, it had to be dead every time — and the law took objection to that. So, to prevent bounty hunters killing the killers, deputy US Marshal Lee Saleen followed when Corrigan and his henchmen set off in pursuit of bank robber and killer Pearly Gillis and his gang. Surrounded by enemies, how would Saleen cope against the overwhelming odds?

MIST RIDER

Luther Chance

Dawn breaks in the town of Random on a bad note. A local man is found dead, hanging from the tree in the livery corral. Worse follows with the discovery of the victims of slaughter and rape at a nearby homestead. Are the two events linked? Who is responsible? Then as Edrow Scoone and his ruthless, tormenting sidekicks make life for the townsfolk a nightmare, a stranger, scarred and silent, books himself a room at the Golden Gaze saloon . . .